Acting Edition

Rodgers & Hammerstein's South Pacific

Music by
Richard Rodgers

Lyrics by
Oscar Hammerstein II

Book by Oscar Hammerstein II & Joshua Logan

Adapted from the Pulitzer Prize-winning novel
Tales of the South Pacific by James A. Michener

CONCORD
THEATRICALS

Copyright © 1949 by Richard Rodgers and Oscar Hammerstein II.
Copyright Renewed. International Copyright Secured.
All Rights Reserved

SOUTH PACIFIC is fully protected under the copyright laws of the United States of America, the British Commonwealth, including Canada, and all member countries of the Berne Convention for the Protection of Literary and Artistic Works, the Universal Copyright Convention, and/or the World Trade Organization conforming to the Agreement on Trade Related Aspects of Intellectual Property Rights. All rights, including professional and amateur stage productions, recitation, lecturing, public reading, motion picture, radio broadcasting, television, online/digital production, and the rights of translation into foreign languages are strictly reserved.

ISBN 978-0-573-70891-6

www.concordtheatricals.com
www.concordtheatricals.co.uk

FOR PRODUCTION INQUIRIES

UNITED STATES AND CANADA
info@concordtheatricals.com
1-866-979-0447

UNITED KINGDOM AND EUROPE
licensing@concordtheatricals.co.uk
020-7054-7298

Each title is subject to availability from Concord Theatricals Corp., depending upon country of performance. Please be aware that *SOUTH PACIFIC* may not be licensed by Concord Theatricals Corp. in your territory. Professional and amateur producers should contact the nearest Concord Theatricals Corp. office or licensing partner to verify availability.

CAUTION: Professional and amateur producers are hereby warned that *SOUTH PACIFIC* is subject to a licensing fee. The purchase, renting, lending or use of this book does not constitute a license to perform this title(s), which license must be obtained from Concord Theatricals Corp. prior to any performance. Performance of this title(s) without a license is a violation of federal law and may subject the producer and/or presenter of such performances to civil penalties. Both amateurs and professionals considering a production are strongly advised to apply to the appropriate agent before starting rehearsals, advertising, or booking a theatre. A licensing fee must be paid whether the title(s) is presented for charity or gain and whether or not admission is charged. Professional/Stock licensing fees are quoted upon application to Concord Theatricals Corp.

This work is published by R&H Theatricals, an imprint of Concord Theatricals Corp.

No one shall make any changes in this title(s) for the purpose of production. No part of this book may be reproduced, stored in a retrieval system, scanned, uploaded, or transmitted in any form, by any means, now known or yet to be invented, including mechanical, electronic, digital, photocopying, recording, videotaping, or otherwise, without the prior written permission of the publisher. No one shall share this title(s), or any part of this title(s), through any social media or file hosting websites.

For all inquiries regarding motion picture, television, online/digital and other media rights, please contact Concord Theatricals Corp.

THIRD-PARTY MATERIALS USE NOTE

Licensees are solely responsible for obtaining formal written permission from copyright owners to use copyrighted third-party materials (e.g., incidental music not provided in connection with a performance license, artworks, logos) in the performance of this play and are strongly cautioned to do so. If no such permission is obtained by the licensee, then the licensee must use only original materials and materials that the licensee owns and controls. Licensees are solely responsible and liable for clearances of all third-party copyrighted materials, and shall indemnify the copyright owners of the play(s) and their licensing agent, Concord Theatricals Corp., against any costs, expenses, losses and liabilities arising from the use of such copyrighted third-party materials by licensees. For music, please contact the appropriate music licensing authority in your territory for the rights to any incidental music not provided in connection with a performance license.

IMPORTANT BILLING AND CREDIT REQUIREMENTS

If you have obtained performance rights to this title, please refer to your licensing agreement for important billing and credit requirements.

SOUTH PACIFIC premiered on Broadway at the Majestic Theatre in New York on April 7, 1949, presented by the Messrs. Rodgers & Hammerstein in association with Leland Hayward and Joshua Logan. The production was directed by Joshua Logan, with scenic and lighting design by Jo Mielziner, costume design by Motley, musical direction by Salvatore Dell'Isola, and orchestrations by Robert Russell Bennett. The cast was as follows:

ENSIGN NELLIE FORBUSH	Mary Martin
EMILE DE BECQUE	Ezio Pinza
NGANA	Barbara Luna
HENRY	Richard Silvera
BLOODY MARY	Juanita Hall
LIAT	Betta St. John
LUTHER BILLIS	Myron McCormick
ABNER	Archie Savage
STEWPOT	Henry Slate
PROFESSOR	Fred Sadoff
LT. JOSEPH CABLE	William Tabbert
CAPT. GEORGE BRACKETT	Martin Wolfson
CMDR. WILLIAM HARBISON	Harvey Stephens
MARINE CORPORAL HAMILTON STEEVES	Jim Hawthorne
LT. BUZZ ADAMS	Don Fellows
LT. GENEVIEVE MARSHALL	Jacqueline Fisher
YEOMAN HEBERT QUALE	Alan Gilbert
RADIO OPERATOR BOB MCCAFFREY	William Biff McGuire
SEAMAN THOMAS HASSINGER	Jack Fontan
SEAMAN JAMES HAYES	Beau Tilden
SEAMAN TOM O'BRIEN	Bill Dwyer
SEABEE MORTON WISE	Henry Michel
SEABEE RICHARD WEST	Dickinson Eastham
SGT. KENNETH JOHNSON	Thomas Gleason
ENSIGN DINAH MURPHY	Roslynd Lowe
ENSIGN JANET MACGREGOR	Sandra Deel
ENSIGN CONNIE WALEWSKA	Mardi Bayne
ENSIGN PAMELA WHITMORE	Evelyn Colby
ENSIGN LISA MINELLI	Gloria Meli
ENSIGN SUE YAEGER	Pat Northrop
ENSIGN CORA MACRAE	Bernice Saunders
ENSIGN BESSIE NOONAN	Helena Schurgot

BLOODY MARY'S ASSISTANT .... Musa Williams
MARCEL / HENRY'S ASSISTANT / ENSEMBLE.............. Richard Loo
ENSEMBLE............................William Ferguson, Alex Nicol,
Mary Ann Reeve, Eugene Smith, Chin Yu

CHARACTERS

ENSIGN NELLIE FORBUSH – a nurse from Arkansas

EMILE DE BECQUE – an expatriate French plantation owner

NGANA – Emile's young, half-Polynesian daughter

JEROME – Emile's young, half-Polynesian son

HENRY – Emile's native servant

BLOODY MARY – a Tonkinese native, expert at trading with the military men

LIAT – Bloody Mary's daughter

BLOODY MARY'S ASSISTANT – Bloody Mary's daughter

LUTHER BILLIS – a sailor

ABNER

STEWPOT (CARPENTER'S MATE, SECOND CLASS GEORGE WATTS)

PROFESSOR – a sailor

LT. JOSEPH CABLE, UNITED STATES MARINE CORPS

CAPT. GEORGE BRACKETT, UNITED STATES NAVY – the highest-ranking officer

CMDR. WILLIAM HARBISON, UNITED STATES NAVY – the second-highest-ranking officer

LT. BUZZ ADAMS

YEOMAN HEBERT QUALE – a sailor

RADIO OPERATOR BOB MCCAFFREY – a sailor

2 SEABEES

2 SAILORS

3 MARINES

A SHORE PATROLMAN

LEAD NURSE (originally named Lt. Genevieve Marshall)

ENSIGN DINAH MURPHY

ENSIGN JANET MACGREGOR

7 ENSIGNS

ENSEMBLE – large singing ensemble consisting of **ISLANDERS, OFFICERS, SAILORS, MARINES, SEABEES,** and **SOLDIERS**

CASTING NOTE

The story takes place in the South Pacific during World War II. The cast includes Americans and people native to the South Pacific. Those characters native to the area should be cast accordingly. The use of makeup or prosthetics to alter an actor's ethnicity is prohibited.

SETTING

The action of the play takes place on two islands in the South Pacific.

TIME

During World War II.
There is one week's lapse of time between the two Acts.

ADDITIONAL SONG

In Act I, Scene Six, an additional song, Music No. 18A "My Girl Back Home," sung by Lt. Cable and Nellie, as well as an adjoining Scene Change music cue, can be added. This additional song insert replaces all dialogue and action on page 44 of this script. Please contact Concord Theatricals to license the music for this song.

AUTHORS' NOTE

NOTES ON THE MILITARY

When *South Pacific* was first produced in 1949, audiences were largely familiar with the military aspects of the show. The further World War II recedes into memory, however, the more unfamiliar the rankings, ratings, machinery, behavior, and feel of wartime military behavior become. By way of assistance we offer this brief guide to the military aspects of the show.

The characters in *South Pacific* have decidedly different ranks. Captain Brackett is the highest-ranking officer, followed by Commander Harbison. They do not salute each other, but everyone else would salute either or both. When Captain Brackett and Commander Harbison first enter, however, [Act I, Scene Three] the men pretend to be preoccupied and do not salute. This might bother the Captain if he weren't so furious at Bloody Mary as not to notice. Joe Cable is a Marine Lieutenant and, as such, merits a salute from the enlisted men which he would return with a salute. He would also salute Captain Brackett and Commander Harbison. When Cable first enters, the men should rise to salute him, but Billis signals them to desist. Luther Billis is a sailor who bullies, bribes, and charms his way through military life, although ultimately he always loses. He has no respect for authority unless he is scared or wants something.

The enlisted men are rated, not ranked. The ratings are Sailors, Marines, and Seabees and differ by their functions in war. Sailors serve at sea, Marines are amphibious troops who serve both on ships and on land, and Seabees are sailors who serve in the Construction Battalion (hence their acronym, C.B.) and are responsible for the construction and maintenance of the bases and their equipment. As the action of *South Pacific* takes place one step removed from the battlefront, there is a decidedly casual aspect to the enlisted men. They are caught in a middle ground – not quite in the war, not quite out of the war.

As for equipment, a PBY was a slow but steady seaplane used mostly for reconnaissance. Jerry cans are large, metal, rectangular cans to hold gasoline or other liquids, frequently seen strapped to the sides of jeeps.

MUSICAL NUMBERS

ACT I

"Opening (Dites-Moi)" .... Ngana & Jerome
"A Cockeyed Optimist" .... Nellie
"Twin Soliloquies" .... Nellie & Emile
"Some Enchanted Evening" .... Emile
"Dites-Moi (Reprise)" .... Ngana, Jerome and Emile
"Bloody Mary" .... Sailors, Seabees, Marines
"There Is Nothin' Like A Dame" .... Billis, Sailors, Seabees, Marines
"Bali Ha'i" .... Bloody Mary
"Cable Hears 'Bali Ha'i'" .... Cable
"I'm Gonna Wash That Man Right
    Outa My Hair" .... Nellie & Nurses
"Some Enchanted Evening (Reprise)" .... Emile & Nellie
"I'm In Love With A Wonderful Guy" .... Nellie & Nurses
"Bali Ha'i (Reprise)" .... French & Native Girls
"Younger Than Springtime" .... Cable
"I'm In Love With A
    Wonderful Guy (Reprise)" .... Nellie & Emile
"This Is How It Feels" .... Nellie & Emile
"I'm Gonna Wash That Man (Encore)" .... Emile
"Finale Act I" .... Emile

ACT II

"Opening Act II" .... Nellie, Nurses, G.I.s
"Happy Talk" .... Bloody Mary & Liat
"Honey Bun" .... Nellie, Billis, Ensemble
"You've Got To Be Carefully Taught" .... Cable
"This Nearly Was Mine" .... Emile
"Some Enchanted Evening (Reprise)" .... Nellie
"Honey Bun (Reprise)" .... All
"Finale Ultimo" .... Nellie, Ngana, Jerome, Emile

NGANA & JEROME.
DITES-MOI
POURQUOI
LA VIE EST BELLE,
DITES-MOI
POURQUOI
LA VIE EST GAIE!
DITES-MOI
POURQUOI,
CHERE MAD'MOISELLE,

    (**NGANA** *curtseys,* **JEROME** *bows.*)

EST-CE QUE
PARCE QUE
VOUS M'AIMEZ?

    (**HENRY,** *a servant, enters from the house and scolds them.*)

HENRY. Allez-vous! Vite! Dans la maison!

NGANA. Non, Henri!

JEROME. *(Mischievously delivering an ultimatum.)* Moi, je reste ici!

HENRY. Oh, oui? Nous verrons bien...

    (*He chases* **JEROME** *around the giggling* **NGANA.**)

Viens, petit moustique!

    (*He catches* **JEROME.** *He is not as angry as he pretends to be, but he grabs* **JEROME** *by the ear and leads him off squealing, followed by* **NGANA,** *who protests violently.*)

NGANA. Non, Henri...non...non!

    (*As she runs off,* **NELLIE** *and* **EMILE** *are heard offstage from around the corner of the house.*)

NELLIE. *(Offstage.)* What's this one?

EMILE. *(Offstage.)* That is frangipani.

NELLIE. *(Offstage.)* But what a color!

EMILE. *(Offstage.)* You will find many more flowers out here.

ACT I

[MUSIC NO. 01 "OVERTURE"]

Scene One
The Terrace of Emile de Becque's Plantation Home

(The terrace of Emile de Becque's plantation home on an island in the South Pacific. Stage left is a one-storied residence. Stage right is a teakwood pagoda at the edge of the cacao grove, on which is placed two teakwood chairs, a coffee table, and a small bench used as a seat behind the table. The house and pagoda are bordered and decked in the bright, tropical colors of the flaming hibiscus, the purple bougainvillaea, and the more pale and delicate frangipani. Between the house and the pagoda you can see the bay below and, on the open sea beyond the bay, the island of Bali Ha'i from which twin volcanoes rise.)

[MUSIC NO. 02 "OPENING (DITES-MOI)"]

*(At Rise: Two Eurasian children – **NGANA**, a girl about eleven, and **JEROME**, a boy about eight – are, with humorous dignity, dancing an impromptu minuet. A bird call is heard in the tree above. **JEROME** looks up and imitates the sound. The eyes of both children follow the flight of the bird. **NGANA** runs over to the pagoda and climbs up on the table and poses on it as if it were a stage. **JEROME** lifts his hands and solemnly conducts while they both sing.)*

(NELLIE enters, looking around her, entranced by the beauty of the scene. She turns upstage to gaze out over the bay. HENRY enters, crossing to a small coffee table with a tray on which are set two large brandy snifters, coffee pot, bottle of brandy, sugar bowl, two demitasse, and sugar tongs. EMILE, entering a few paces behind NELLIE, crosses and addresses HENRY.)

Je servirai le café.

HENRY. Oui, Monsieur.

EMILE. C'est tout.

HENRY. Oui, Monsieur de Becque.

(He exits into the house.)

NELLIE. *(Crossing to EMILE.)* Well, I'm just speechless! … And that lunch! Wild chicken – I didn't know it was ever wild. Gosh! I had no idea that people lived like this right out in the middle of the Pacific Ocean.

EMILE. *(Pouring coffee.)* Sugar?

NELLIE. Thanks.

EMILE. One?

NELLIE. Three.

(EMILE looks up, then puts two lumps of sugar in the cup.)

I know it's a big load for a demitasse to carry.

(EMILE puts a third lump of sugar in the cup.)

All right, I'm a hick. You know so many American words, do you know what a hick is?

EMILE. A hick is one who lives in a stick.

NELLIE. Sticks. Plural. *The* sticks.

EMILE. Pardon. *The* sticks. I remember now.

(He hands NELLIE the coffee cup.)

NELLIE. How long did it take you to build up a plantation like this?

EMILE. I came to the Pacific when I was a young man.

NELLIE. Emile, is it true that all the planters on these islands – are they all running away from something?

EMILE. *(Pausing briefly, cautious in his answer.)* Who is not running away from something? There are fugitives everywhere – Paris, New York, even in Small Rock...

>*(**NELLIE** looks puzzled.)*

Where you come from...

NELLIE. *(Suddenly understanding what he means, she bursts out laughing.)* Oh, *Little* Rock!

EMILE. *(Laughing with her and shouting the correction.)* *Little* Rock! ...You know fugitives there?

>*(**NELLIE** runs over to where she has left her bag.)*

NELLIE. I'll show you a picture of a Little Rock fugitive.

>*(Taking an envelope from the bag.)*

I got this clipping from my mother today.

>*(She hands it to **EMILE**, who reads.)*

EMILE. "Ensign Nellie Forbush, Arkansas' own Florence Nightingale..."

NELLIE. *(Apologetically.)* That was written by Mrs. Leeming, the social editor. She went to school with my mother. To read her, you'd think that I'm practically the most important nurse in the entire Navy and that it's only a matter of time before I become a lady admiral.

EMILE. In this picture you do not look much like an admiral.

NELLIE. Oh, that was taken before I knew what rain and heat and mud could do to your disposition.

>*(**EMILE** looks fixedly at her. She, embarrassed, cannot meet his gaze, turns and crosses.)*

But it isn't rainy today. Gosh, it's beautiful here.

[MUSIC NO. 03 "MUSIC UNDER SCENE"]

Just look at that yellow sun! You know, I don't think it's the end of the world like everyone else thinks. I just can't work myself *up* to getting that *low*.

(EMILE smiles.)

Do you think I'm crazy too? They all do over at the fleet hospital.

[MUSIC NO. 04 "A COCKEYED OPTIMIST"]

You know what they call me? Knucklehead Nellie. I suppose I am, but I can't help it.

WHEN THE SKY IS A BRIGHT CANARY YELLOW
I FORGET EVERY CLOUD I'VE EVER SEEN –
SO THEY CALL ME A COCKEYED OPTIMIST,
IMMATURE AND INCURABLY GREEN!

I HAVE HEARD PEOPLE RANT AND RAVE AND BELLOW
THAT WE'RE DONE AND WE MIGHT AS WELL BE DEAD –
BUT I'M ONLY A COCKEYED OPTIMIST,
AND I CAN'T GET IT INTO MY HEAD.

I HEAR THE HUMAN RACE
IS FALLING ON ITS FACE
AND HASN'T VERY FAR TO GO,
BUT EVERY WHIPPOORWILL
IS SELLING ME A BILL
AND TELLING ME IT JUST AIN'T SO!

I COULD SAY LIFE IS JUST A BOWL OF JELLO,
AND APPEAR MORE INTELLIGENT AND SMART
BUT I'M STUCK
(LIKE A DOPE!)
WITH A THING CALLED HOPE,
AND I CAN'T GET IT OUT OF MY HEART...
NOT THIS HEART!

(She crosses to EMILE, continuing.)

Wanna know anything else about me?

EMILE. Yes. You say you are a fugitive. When you joined the Navy, what were *you* running away from?

[MUSIC NO. 05 "THE SCENE CONTINUES"]

(He returns the clipping to NELLIE.)

NELLIE. Gosh, I don't know. It was more like I was running to something. I wanted to see what the world was like – outside Little Rock, I mean. And I wanted to meet different kinds of people and find out if I like them better.

> *(She turns, looks at* **EMILE***, notices that he is looking at her, and she suddenly become self-conscious. She turns and looks front.)*

And I'm finding out.

EMILE. *(Tactfully.)* Would you like some cognac?

NELLIE. *(Relieved.)* I'd love some.

[MUSIC NO. 06 "TWIN SOLILOQUIES"]

> *(She replaces the clipping in her bag and watches* **EMILE** *thoughtfully. He goes to the table to pour the brandy. In the following verses,* **EMILE** *and* **NELLIE** *are not singing to each other – each is soliloquizing.)*

WONDER HOW I'D FEEL,
LIVING ON A HILLSIDE,
LOOKING ON AN OCEAN
BEAUTIFUL AND STILL.

EMILE.

THIS IS WHAT I NEED,
THIS IS WHAT I'VE LONGED FOR,
SOMEONE YOUNG AND SMILING
CLIMBING UP MY HILL!

NELLIE. *(Turning toward* **EMILE***. He is pouring the brandy.)*

WE ARE NOT ALIKE;
PROBABLY I'D BORE HIM.
HE'S A CULTURED FRENCHMAN –
I'M A LITTLE HICK.

EMILE. *(Pausing as he starts to pour the second glass.)*

YOUNGER MEN THAN I,
OFFICERS AND DOCTORS,
PROBABLY PURSUE HER –
SHE COULD HAVE HER PICK.

> *(***NELLIE** *catches his eye. They exchange a quick look. Each averts their eyes from the other as* **EMILE** *corks the bottle and replaces it on the tray.)*

NELLIE.
>WONDER WHY I FEEL
>JITTERY AND JUMPY!
>I AM LIKE A SCHOOLGIRL,
>WAITING FOR A DANCE.

EMILE. *(Picking up the two filled brandy snifters.)*
>CAN I ASK HER NOW?
>I AM LIKE A SCHOOLBOY!
>WHAT WILL BE HER ANSWER?
>DO I HAVE A CHANCE?

>*(He approaches **NELLIE** as the music segues to:)*

[MUSIC NO. 07 "UNSPOKEN THOUGHTS"]

>*(He passes **NELLIE** her snifter. She has apparently never drunk from one before. She watches him carefully as he warms his brandy, holding the snifter in the palms of both hands and making a gentle circular motion. She does the same. As they drink, the music rises to great ecstatic heights. One is made aware that in this simple act of two people falling in love, each drinking brandy, there are turbulent thoughts and feelings going on in their hearts and brains. They lower their glasses; the music dies down. **EMILE** struggles to say something. He plunges into the middle of his subject as if continuing a thought which he assumes she has sensed.)*

In peacetime, the boat from America comes once a month. The ladies – the wives of the planters – often go to Australia during the hot months. It can get very hot here.

NELLIE. *(Immediately.)* It can get hot in Arkansas, too.

>*(She takes another quick swallow.)*

EMILE. Ah, yes?

NELLIE. *(Nodding her head.)* Uh-huh.

(She takes another quick sip.)

EMILE. *(Puts his glass down on the table.)* I have many books here... Marcel Proust?

> *(**NELLIE** looks blank.)*

André Gide?

> *(This evokes a faint smile of half-recognition from **NELLIE**.)*

Did you study French in school?

NELLIE. Oh, yes.

EMILE. Ah, then you can read French?

NELLIE. *(As though saying, "Of course not.")* No!
(A feeble attempt to add a note of hope.) I can conjugate a few verbs.

> *(Realizing how silly this must sound to him, she changes the subject.)*

I bet you read a lot.

EMILE. Out here, one becomes hungry to learn everything.

> *(He rises and paces pensively.)*

Not to miss anything, not to let anything good pass by.

> *(He pauses and looks down at **NELLIE**.)*

NELLIE. Yes?

EMILE. One waits so long for what is good...and when at last it comes, one cannot risk to lose.

> *(He turns away, searching for more words.)*

So...so one must speak and act quickly...

[MUSIC NO. 08 "INTRO TO 'SOME ENCHANTED EVENING'"]

...even...even if it seems almost foolish to be so quick.

> *(He has gone too far to stop now.)*

I know it is only two weeks. A dinner given at your Officers' Club. Do you remember?

NELLIE. Yes.

EMILE And that is the way things happen sometimes... Isn't it, Nellie?

NELLIE. *(Swallowing hard.)* Yes, it is...Emile.

[MUSIC NO. 09 "SOME ENCHANTED EVENING"]

EMILE.
>SOME ENCHANTED EVENING
>YOU MAY SEE A STRANGER,
>YOU MAY SEE A STRANGER
>ACROSS A CROWDED ROOM.
>AND SOMEHOW YOU KNOW,
>YOU KNOW EVEN THEN,
>THAT SOMEWHERE YOU'LL SEE HER AGAIN AND AGAIN.
>
>SOME ENCHANTED EVENING
>SOMEONE MAY BE LAUGHING,
>YOU MAY HEAR HER LAUGHING
>ACROSS A CROWDED ROOM –
>AND NIGHT AFTER NIGHT,
>AS STRANGE AS IT SEEMS,
>THE SOUND OF HER LAUGHTER WILL SING IN YOUR DREAMS.
>
>WHO CAN EXPLAIN IT?
>WHO CAN TELL YOU WHY?
>FOOLS GIVE YOU REASONS –
>WISE MEN NEVER TRY.
>
>SOME ENCHANTED EVENING,
>WHEN YOU FIND YOUR TRUE LOVE,
>WHEN YOU FEEL HER CALL YOU
>ACROSS A CROWDED ROOM –
>THEN FLY TO HER SIDE
>AND MAKE HER YOUR OWN,
>OR ALL THROUGH YOUR LIFE YOU MAY DREAM ALL ALONE.
>
>ONCE YOU HAVE FOUND HER,
>NEVER LET HER GO.
>ONCE YOU HAVE FOUND HER,
>NEVER LET HER GO!

[MUSIC NO. 10 "SOME ENCHANTED EVENING (ENCORE)"]

EMILE.
>SOME ENCHANTED EVENING,
>WHEN YOU FIND YOUR TRUE LOVE,
>WHEN YOU FEEL HER CALL YOU
>ACROSS A CROWDED ROOM –

>*(There follow several seconds of silence. Neither moves. **EMILE** speaks over the music.)*

I am older than you. If we have children, when I die they will be growing up. You could afford to take them back to America – if you like. Think about it.

>*(**HENRY** enters from the house.)*

HENRY. Monsieur de Becque, la zheep de Mademoiselle est ici.

>*(**EMILE** and **NELLIE** turn as if awakened from a dream.)*

La zheep de Mademoiselle.

>*(**NELLIE** turns to **HENRY**.)*

Votre zheep!

>*(He smiles and indicates with both hands as if steering.)*

NELLIE. My "zheep"? Oh, my jeep!

>*(She looks at her watch.)*

Gosh! Thank you, Henry. I'm on duty in ten minutes!

>*(**HENRY** exits. **NELLIE** holds out her hand to **EMILE**.)*

EMILE. Before you leave, Nellie, I want to tell you something. A while ago, you asked me a question – why did I leave France?

NELLIE. Oh, Emile, that was none of my business.

EMILE. But I want to tell you. I had to leave France. I killed a man.

>*(Pause.)*

NELLIE. Why did you kill him?

EMILE. He was a wicked man, a bully. Everyone in our village was glad to see him die. It was not to my discredit. Do you believe me, Nellie?

> *(Another pause, unbearable to him.)*

NELLIE. You have just told me that you killed a man and that it's all right. I hardly know you, and yet I know it's all right.

EMILE. *(Deeply moved.)* Thank you, Nellie.

> *(His voice suddenly exultant.)* Do you like my place?

NELLIE. Yes.

EMILE. You will think?

NELLIE. *(Smiling up at him.)* I will think.

> *(They are silent and motionless for a moment. Then **NELLIE** turns and suddenly walks off very quickly. **EMILE** looks after her and starts to hum softly. He picks up the demitasse she has left on the fountain and smiles down at it. He holds the cup up so he can examine its rim.)*

EMILE. Lipstick! ...Three lumps of sugar in this little cup!

> *(He laughs aloud, then resumes his humming and walks, almost dances, across the stage to the table in time to his own music. **NGANA** and **JEROME** enter from the house and walk behind him across the stage, imitating his happy stride. As **EMILE** puts down the cup, the **CHILDREN** join him, humming the same melody. He turns quickly and frowns down on them with mock sternness. They giggle.)*

Eh bien!

JEROME. Bravo, Papa!

> *(The **CHILDREN** both applaud.)*

EMILE. Merci, Monsieur!

NGANA. Nous chantons bien, aussi.

[MUSIC NO. 11 "DITES-MOI (REPRISE)"]

EMILE. Ah, oui?

NGANA. Attends, Papa!

JEROME. *(Parroting* **NGANA.***)* Attends, Papa!

>*(He looks at **NGANA** for the signal to start the song. They sing...**EMILE** conducting them.)*

NGANA & JEROME.
>DITES-MOI
>POURQUOI
>LA VIE EST BELLE,

EMILE, NGANA & JEROME.
>DITES-MOI
>POURQUOI
>LA VIE EST GAIE!
>
>DITES-MOI
>POURQUOI,

>*(**EMILE** and **JEROME** make a deep bow to **NGANA**.)*

CHERE MAD'MOISELLE,

>*(**EMILE** picks them up, one under each arm, and starts to carry them off as they finish singing the refrain together.)*

EST-CE QUE
PARCE QUE
VOUS M'AIMEZ?

[MUSIC NO. 12 "BLOODY MARY"]

>*(Happening almost simultaneously is the following: the lights fade out quickly, a scrim traveler closes downstage, and, in the dark, **SAILORS**, **SEABEES**, and **MARINES** run on very quickly, singing the beginning of "Bloody Mary." The lights then snap up suddenly, revealing the traveler which represents no specific place, but rather a pattern of a large tapa-cloth.)*

Scene Two
Another Part of the Island

MEN. *(Entering.)*
BLOODY MARY IS THE GIRL I LOVE,
BLOODY MARY IS THE GIRL I LOVE,
BLOODY MARY IS THE GIRL I LOVE –
NOW AIN'T THAT TOO DAMN BAD!

HER SKIN IS TENDER AS DIMAGGIO'S GLOVE,
HER SKIN IS TENDER AS DIMAGGIO'S GLOVE,
HER SKIN IS TENDER AS DIMAGGIO'S GLOVE –
NOW AIN'T THAT TOO DAMN BAD!

*(The music stops. The object of this serenade has been hidden during the song by some **SAILORS** and is now revealed as they move away. This is **BLOODY MARY**. She is a Tonkinese trader. She wears black sateen trousers and a white blouse over which is an old Marine's tunic. On her head is a peach-basket hat. Around her neck is a G.I. identification chain from which hangs a silver Marine emblem. At the end of the singing, she gives out a shrill cackle of laughter with which we shall soon learn to identify her.)*

BLOODY MARY. *(Looking straight out at the audience.)* Hallo, G.I.!

(She holds up a grass skirt.)

Grass skirt? Very saxy! Fo'dolla'? Saxy grass skirt. Fo'dolla'! Send home Chicago. You like? You buy?

(Her eyes scan the audience as if following a passerby. Her crafty smile fades to a quick scowl as he apparently passes without buying. She calls after him.)

Where you go? Come back! Chipskate! Crummy G.I.! Sadsack. Droopy-drawers!

MARINE. Tell 'em good, Mary!

BLOODY MARY. What is good?

MARINE. Tell him he's a stingy bastard!

BLOODY MARY. *(Delighted at the sound of these new words.)* Stingy bastard!

> *(She turns back toward the **MARINE** for approval.)*

That good?

MARINE. That's great, Mary! You're learning fast.

BLOODY MARY. *(Calling off again.)* Stingy bastard!

> *(She cackles gaily and turns to the **MARINE**.)*

I learn fast – pretty soon I talk English good as any crummy Marine.

(Calling off once more.) Stingy bastard!

> *(She cackles very loudly, but the **MARINES**, **SEABEES**, and **SAILORS** laugh louder and cheer her. The lights behind the traveler come up as they resume their serenade.)*

MEN.
BLOODY MARY'S CHEWING BETEL NUTS,
SHE IS ALWAYS CHEWING BETEL NUTS,
BLOODY MARY'S CHEWING BETEL NUTS –
AND SHE DON'T USE PEPSODENT!

> *(**BLOODY MARY** grins and shows her betel-stained teeth.)*

NOW AIN'T THAT TOO DAMN BAD!

Scene Three
The Edge of a Palm Grove Near the Beach

(The edge of a palm grove near the beach. Beyond can be seen the beach, the bay, the open sea, and Bali Ha'i. Stage right is Bloody Mary's kiosk. This is made of bamboo and canvas and is portable and collapsible. Her merchandise, laid out in front, comprises shells, native straw hats, local dress material, toy outrigger canoes, and hookahs. Several grass skirts are hanging up around the kiosk. Stage left, at first making a puzzling silhouette, then as the lights come up, revealing itself to be a contraption of weird detail, is a G.I. homemade washing machine. It looks partly like a giant ice-cream freezer, partly like a windmill. In front of it there is a sign which reads:)

"TWISTED AIR HAND LAUNDRY
LUTHER BILLIS ENTERPRISES
SPECIAL RATES FOR SEABEES"

(As the lights come up, the washing machine is being operated by Carpenter's Mate, Second Class George Watts, better known as **STEWPOT. SEABEES, SAILORS, MARINES,** *and some* **ARMY MEN** *lounge around the scene waiting for whatever diversion* **BLOODY MARY** *may provide. Also present is* **BLOODY MARY'S ASSISTANT.** *During the singing that covers this change,* **BLOODY MARY** *takes a strange-looking object out of her pocket and dangles it in front of a sailor,* **O'BRIEN.***)*

O'BRIEN. What is that thing?

BLOODY MARY. *(Holding the small object in her hand.)* Is head. Fifty dolla'.

O'BRIEN. *(Revolted.)* What's it *made* of?

BLOODY MARY. Made outa head! Is real human.

O'BRIEN. *(Skeptical.)* What makes it so small?

BLOODY MARY. Shlunk!

> *(She puts head between hands and squeezes it.)*

Only way to keep human head is shlink 'em.

O'BRIEN. No, thanks.

> *(He leaves quickly.)*

BLOODY MARY. *(To a new customer as she holds a grass skirt up to her waist and starts to dance.)* Fo' dolla'. Send home Chicago to saxy sweetheart! She make wave like this.

> *(Music continues as she starts to dance. One of the* **SAILORS** *grabs her and goes into an impromptu jitterbug dance with her. Others join, and soon the beach is alive with gyrating gentlemen of the United States Armed Services. As this spontaneous festivity is at its height,* **LUTHER BILLIS** *enters, followed by the* **PROFESSOR**, *both loaded with grass skirts. They come down in front of* **BLOODY MARY** *and throw the grass skirts at her feet.)*

BILLIS. Here you are, Sweaty Pie! Put them down, Professor. These beautiful skirts were made by myself, the Professor here, and three other Seabees in half the time it takes your native workers to make 'em.

> *(He picks up a skirt and demonstrates.)*

See? No stretch!

> *(Throwing the skirt back on the ground.)*

Look 'em over, Sweaty Pie, and give me your price.

> *(At this point, an altercation starts upstage near the washing machine.)*

SAILOR. Look at that shirt!

STEWPOT. Take it up with the manager.

> *(He points down to* **BILLIS.***)*

SAILOR. *(Coming down to him.)* Hey, Big Dealer! Hey, Luther Billis!

BILLIS. *(Smoothly.)* What can I do for you, my boy? What's the trouble?

SAILOR. *(Holding up his shirt, which has been laundered and is in tatters.)* Look at that shirt!

BILLIS. The Billis Laundry is not responsible for minor burns and tears.

> *(He turns back laconically to* **BLOODY MARY.***)*

What do you say, Sweatso? What am I offered?

> *(The* **SAILOR** *hurls his shirt at a surprised* **STEWPOT.** *The* **PROFESSOR,** *meanwhile, is showing the beautiful work they do to some other* **SAILORS** *and* **SEABEES.***)*

PROFESSOR. *(Holding up a skirt.)* All handsewn!

QUALE. Gee, that's mighty nice work!

BILLIS. *(To* **BLOODY MARY,** *confidentially.)* Do you hear that, Sweaty Pie? You can probably sell these to the chumps for five or six dollars apiece. Now, I'll let you have the whole bunch for...say...eighty bucks.

BLOODY MARY. Give you ten dolla'.

BILLIS. What?

BLOODY MARY. Not enough?

BILLIS. You're damn well right, not enough!

BLOODY MARY. *(Dropping the skirt at his feet.)* Den you damn well keep.

> *(She goes down to another* **SAILOR** *and takes from her pocket a boar's-tooth bracelet, which she holds up to tempt him.)*

BILLIS. *(Following* **BLOODY MARY.***)* Now look here, Dragon Lady...

> *(Whatever he was about to say is knocked out of his head by the sight of the bracelet.* **BILLIS** *is an inveterate and passionate souvenir hunter.)*

BILLIS. What's that you got there? A boar's-tooth bracelet? Where'd you get that?

> *(She points to the twin-peaked island.)*

Over there on Bali Ha'i?

BLOODY MARY. *(Smiling craftily.)* You like?

BILLIS. *(Taking bracelet and showing it to* **G.I.S** *who have huddled around him.)* You know what that is? A bracelet made out of a single boar's tooth. They cut the tooth from the boar's mouth in a big ceremonial over there on Bali Ha'i. There ain't a souvenir you can pick up in the South Pacific as valuable as this...

(To **BLOODY MARY**.*)* What do you want for it, Mary?

BLOODY MARY. Hundred dolla'!

BILLIS. Hundred dollars!

> *(Shocked, but realizing he will pay it, he turns to the* **PROFESSOR** *and* **STEWPOT** *and takes money from his pocket.)*

That's cheap. I thought it would be more.

PROFESSOR. I don't see how she can turn them out for that.

BLOODY MARY. Make you special offer Big Deala. I trade you boar's-tooth bracelet for all grass skirts.

BILLIS. *(Grabs skirts from the* **PROFESSOR**, *throws them at* **BLOODY MARY**'s *feet.)* It's a deal.

BLOODY MARY. Wait a minute. Is no deal till you throw in something for good luck.

BILLIS. Okay. What do you want me to throw in?

BLOODY MARY. *(Taking money from one of his hands, shakes the other one.)* Hundred dolla'. Good luck!

> *(She exits with the grass skirts. The* **MEN** *all crowd around* **BILLIS**, *shaking his hand in ironic "congratulations.")*

BILLIS. You don't run into these things every day. They're scarce as hens' teeth.

PROFESSOR. They're bigger, too.

BILLIS. That damned Bali Ha'i!

(Turning and looking toward the island.)

Why does it have to be off limits? You can get everything over there. Shrunken heads, bracelets, old ivory...

SAILOR. Young French women!

BILLIS. Knock it off! I'm talking about souvenirs.

PROFESSOR. So's he.

BILLIS. *(Pacing restlessly.)* We got to get a boat and get over there. I'm feeling held down again. I need to take a trip.

STEWPOT. Only officers can sign out boats.

BILLIS. I'll get a boat all right. I'll latch onto some officer who's got some imagination – that would like to see that boar's-tooth ceremonial as much as I would. It's a hell of a ceremonial! Dancin', drinkin' – everything!

SAILOR. Why, you big phony. We all know why you want to go to Bali Ha'i.

BILLIS. Why?

SAILOR. Because the French planters put all their young women over there when they heard the G.I.s were coming. That's why! It ain't boars' teeth – it's women!

[MUSIC NO. 13 "THERE IS NOTHIN' LIKE A DAME"]

BILLIS. It is boars' teeth – and women!

(A long pause. At first the MEN are still and thoughtful, each dreaming a similar dream – but his own. Slowly and individually they begin pacing. The movement is not unlike a group of caged animals, each eager to break out. Solo lines are sung out front, not to anyone onstage.)

SAILOR.
WE GOT SUNLIGHT ON THE SAND,
WE GOT MOONLIGHT ON THE SEA,

SEABEE.
>WE GOT MANGOES AND BANANAS
>YOU CAN PICK RIGHT OFF A TREE,

SAILOR.
>WE GOT VOLLEYBALL AND PING-PONG
>AND A LOT OF DANDY GAMES –

BILLIS.
>WHAT *AIN'T* WE GOT?

ALL.
>WE AIN'T GOT DAMES!

MARINE.
>WE GET PACKAGES FROM HOME,

SAILOR.
>WE GET MOVIES, WE GET SHOWS,

STEWPOT.
>WE GET SPEECHES FROM OUR SKIPPER

SOLDIER.
>AND ADVICE FROM TOKYO ROSE,

SEABEE.
>WE GET LETTERS DOUSED WIT' POIFUME,

SAILOR.
>WE GET DIZZY FROM THE SMELL –

BILLIS.
>WHAT *DON'T* WE GET?

ALL.
>YOU KNOW DAMN WELL!

BILLIS. *(Like a recitative.)*
>WE GOT NOTHIN' TO PUT ON A CLEAN, WHITE SUIT FOR.
>WHAT WE NEED IS WHAT THERE AIN'T NO SUBSTITUTE
>>FOR!

ALL.
>THERE IS NOTHIN' LIKE A DAME –
>NOTHIN' IN THE WORLD!
>THERE IS NOTHIN' YOU CAN NAME
>THAT IS ANYTHIN' LIKE A DAME.

MARINE.
>WE FEEL RESTLESS,
>WE FEEL BLUE,

SEABEE.
>WE FEEL LONELY AND, IN BRIEF,
>WE FEEL EVERY KIND OF FEELIN'

PROFESSOR.
>BUT THE FEELIN' OF RELIEF.

SAILOR.
>WE FEEL HUNGRY AS THE WOLF FELT
>WHEN HE MET RED RIDING HOOD –

ALL.
>WHAT *DON'T* WE FEEL?

STEWPOT.
>WE DON'T FEEL GOOD!

BILLIS.
>LOTS OF THINGS IN LIFE ARE BEAUTIFUL, BUT, BROTHER, THERE IS ONE PARTICULAR THING THAT IS NOTHIN' WHATSOEVER IN ANY WAY, SHAPE OR FORM LIKE ANY OTHER.

ALL.
>THERE IS NOTHIN' LIKE A DAME –
>NOTHIN' IN THE WORLD!
>THERE IS NOTHIN' YOU CAN NAME
>THAT IS ANYTHIN' LIKE A DAME.
>
>NOTHIN' ELSE IS BUILT THE SAME!
>NOTHIN' IN THE WORLD

TENOR SOLO.
>HAS A SOFT AND WAVY FRAME
>LIKE THE SILHOUETTE OF A DAME.

BASS SOLO.
>THERE IS ABSOLUTELY NOTHIN' LIKE THE FRAME OF A DAME!

>*(Dialogue continues over tremolo.)*

LEAD NURSE. *(Offstage.)* Hut, two, three, four! Get – your – exercise!

(The husky **LEAD NURSE** *enters, leading several other* **NURSES**, *all dressed in bathing suits, playsuits, or fatigues.* **NELLIE** *is among them. They jog across the stage, their* **LEADER** *continuing the military count. The* **MEN**'s *eyes follow them. Music holds throughout.)*

TIRED NURSE. Can't we rest a while?

LEAD NURSE. Come on you nurses, pick it up!

*(***NELLIE*** drops out of line as the others run off.)*

NELLIE. Hey, Luther!

STEWPOT. *(Nudging* **BILLIS**.*)* Luther!

*(***BILLIS*** turns and goes shyly to* **NELLIE**, *terribly embarrassed that the* **MEN** *are watching him. He is a different* **BILLIS** *in front of* **NELLIE**. *He is unassured and has lost all of his brashness. To him,* **NELLIE** *has "class.")*

BILLIS. Yes, Miss Forbush.

(All eyes follow him.)

NELLIE. Have you done what you promised?

BILLIS. Yes, Miss Forbush.

(He pulls out a newspaper package from a hiding place in the roots of a tree and hands it to **NELLIE**.*)*

I did it all last night.

(With an alarmed look at his comrades, as **NELLIE** *starts to unwrap it.)*

You don't have to open it now.

(But **NELLIE** *opens the package, much to* **BILLIS**' *embarrassment. It is her laundry, neatly folded.)*

NELLIE. *(Holds up a pair of polka-dot underpants.)* Oh. You do beautiful work, Luther!

(*Two* **MEN** *painfully cling to each other and turn their heads away.* **BILLIS** *tries to outglare the others in defensive defiance.*)

You've even done the pleats in my shorts!

BILLIS. Aw, pleats ain't hard. You better run along now and catch up to your gang.

NELLIE. Pleats are *very* hard. How do you do such delicate work at night, in the dark?

BILLIS. There was a moon!

STEWPOT. (*In a syrupy voice.*) There was a moon!

BILLIS. (*Turns to the* **MEN**, *realizing that they have heard this, and shouts defiantly.*) A full moon!

NELLIE. (*Wrapping up the package.*) How much, Luther?

BILLIS. (*Earnestly.*) Oh, no, not from you.

NELLIE. Gosh, I guess I'm just about the luckiest nurse on this island to have found you.

(*She takes his arm.*)

You're a treasure.

(*She notices the* **MEN** *ogling her; embarrassed.*)

Well, good-bye, Luther.

(*She turns and runs off.*)

Hut, two, three, four!

(**BILLIS** *turns abruptly and faces the* **MEN**, *trying to bluff it out. He walks belligerently over to* **STEWPOT**, *who with the* **PROFESSOR** *whistles "There is Nothin' Like a Dame." Then he walks over to another group and they join in whistling. Soon* **ALL** *are whistling.* **BILLIS** *whistles too. After the refrain is finished,* **STEWPOT** *looks off reflectively at the departing* **NELLIE**.)

STEWPOT. She's a nice little girl, but some of them nurses – the officers can have them.

PROFESSOR. They got 'em!
STEWPOT. Well, they can have 'em!
MARINE.
>SO SUPPOSE A DAME AIN'T BRIGHT,
>OR COMPLETELY FREE FROM FLAWS,

SAILOR.
>OR AS FAITHFUL AS A BIRD DOG,

SEABEE.
>OR AS KIND AS SANTA CLAUS –

SOLDIER.
>IT'S A WASTE OF TIME TO WORRY
>OVER THINGS THAT THEY HAVE NOT;

SAILOR.
>BE THANKFUL FOR

ALL.
>THE THINGS THEY GOT!

LEAD NURSE. *(Entering, leading the NURSES in the opposite direction to their previous course.)* Hut, two, three, four! Hut, two, three, four!

>*(NELLIE is at the end of the group. She waves to BILLIS and points to the laundry under her arm. The MEN all rise and turn, their heads following the NURSES until they're off. Then they continue to turn until they're facing front again.)*

ALL.
>THERE IS NOTHIN' YOU CAN NAME
>THAT IS ANYTHIN' LIKE A DAME!
>
>>*(Pacing up and downstage in an irregular formation.)*
>
>THERE ARE NO BOOKS LIKE A DAME
>AND NOTHIN' LOOKS LIKE A DAME.
>THERE ARE NO DRINKS LIKE A DAME
>AND NOTHIN' THINKS LIKE A DAME,
>NOTHIN' ACTS LIKE A DAME
>OR ATTRACTS LIKE A DAME.

THERE AIN'T A THING THAT'S WRONG WITH ANY MAN HERE
THAT CAN'T BE CURED BY PUTTIN' HIM NEAR
A GIRLY, WOMANLY, FEMALE, FEMININE
DAME!

(Music stops, then continues after applause as the MEN resume their inactivity. BLOODY MARY enters, followed by her ASSISTANT, and proceeds to rearrange her new stock of grass skirts.)

BLOODY MARY. *(Humming.)*
THERE IS NOTHIN' YOU CAN NAME
THAT IS ANYTHIN'...

(She sees LIEUTENANT JOSEPH CABLE enter. Music stops. He wears suntans, overseas cap, and carries a musette bag in his hand. They stand for a moment, looking at each other – she, suspicious and frightened, and he, puzzled and curious. The PROFESSOR and one or two others start to rise because a lieutenant is meant to be saluted. BILLIS indicates for them to relax.)

Hallo.

CABLE. Hello.

BLOODY MARY. You mak' trouble for me?

CABLE. Hunh?

BLOODY MARY. Are you crummy Major?

CABLE. No, I'm even crummier than that. I'm a Lieutenant.

BLOODY MARY. Lootellan?

CABLE. *(Laughing.)* Lootellan.

[MUSIC NO. 14 "MARY AND LOOTELLAN"]

(BLOODY MARY stares at CABLE.)

BILLIS. Hiya, Lootellan. New on the rock?

CABLE. Just came in on that PBY.

BILLIS. Yeah? Where from?

CABLE. A little island south of Marie Louise.

> *(Some of the MEN whistle – "hot stuff.")*

STEWPOT. Then you been up where they use real bullets!

CABLE. Unh-huh.

BLOODY MARY. *(Who has been looking adoringly at CABLE.)* Hey, Lootellan. You damn saxy man!

CABLE. *(Rocked off balance for a moment.)* Thanks. You're looking pretty...er...fit yourself.

BLOODY MARY. *(Grins happily at him, turns to her ASSISTANT.)* Damn saxy!

CABLE. *(To BILLIS.)* Who is she?

BILLIS. She's Tonkinese – used to work for a French planter.

BLOODY MARY. French planters stingy bastards!

> *(She laughs.)*

CABLE. Say, I wonder if any of you know a French planter named de Becque?

BILLIS. Emile de Becque? I think he's the guy lives on top of that hill... Do you know him?

CABLE. *(Looking toward the hill, thoughtfully.)* No, but I'm going to.

BLOODY MARY. *(Following CABLE, taking the shrunken head from her pocket.)* Hey, Lootellan.

> *(Music resumes. CABLE turns to her.)*

Real human head! You got sweetheart? Send home Chicago to saxy sweetheart!

CABLE. No – er...she's a Philadelphia girl.

BLOODY MARY. Whazzat, Philadelia girl? Whazzat mean? No saxy?

(With a sudden impulse.) You like I give you free?

BILLIS. Free! You never give *me* anything free.

BLOODY MARY. You not saxy like Lootellan.

(To CABLE, proffering the shrunken head.) Take!

CABLE. No, thanks. Where'd you get that anyway?

BLOODY MARY. Bali Ha'i.

STEWPOT. *(Nudging* **BILLIS**, *pointing to* **CABLE** *as he whispers.)* There's your officer! There's your officer!

BILLIS. That's the island over there with the two volcanoes. *(Significantly.)* Officers can get launches and go over there.

(Music resumes.)

CABLE. *(Looking out at island.)* Bali Ha'i... What does that mean?

BLOODY MARY. Bali Ha'i mean "I am your special island" – mean "Here I am." Bali Ha'i is *your* special island, Lootellan. I know! You listen! You hear island call to you. Listen! You hear something? Listen!

CABLE. *(After listening for a moment.)* I hear the sound of the wind and the waves, that's all.

BLOODY MARY. You no hear something calling? Listen!

(Silence. All listen. Long pause.)

STEWPOT. I think I hear something.

BILLIS. *(In a harsh, threatening whisper.)* Shut your big fat mouth!

BLOODY MARY. Hear voice?

[MUSIC NO. 15 "BALI HA'I"]

(She sings to **CABLE** *as he gazes at the mysterious island.)*

MOS' PEOPLE LIVE ON A LONELY ISLAND,
LOST IN DE MIDDLE OF A FOGGY SEA.
MOS' PEOPLE LONG FOR ANUDDER ISLAND
ONE WHERE DEY KNOW DEY WOULD LAK TO BE...

BALI HA'I
MAY CALL YOU,
ANY NIGHT, ANY DAY
IN YOUR HEART
YOU'LL HEAR IT CALL YOU:
"COME AWAY, COME AWAY."

BALI HA'I
WILL WHISPER

ON DE WIND OF DE SEA:
"HERE AM I,
YOUR SPECIAL ISLAND!
COME TO ME, COME TO ME!"

YOUR OWN SPECIAL HOPES,
YOUR OWN SPECIAL DREAMS,
BLOOM ON DE HILLSIDE
AND SHINE IN DE STREAMS.

IF YOU TRY,
YOU'LL FIND ME
WHERE DE SKY MEETS DE SEA:
"HERE AM I,
YOUR SPECIAL ISLAND!
COME TO ME, COME TO ME!"

BALI HA'I,
BALI HA'I,
BALI HA'I.

>*(The* **MEN** *slowly turn upstage, one by one, to face Bali Ha'i.)*

SOMEDAY YOU'LL SEE ME,
FLOATIN' IN DE SUNSHINE,
MY HEAD STICKIN' OUT
F'UM A LOW-FLYIN' CLOUD;
YOU'LL HEAR ME CALL YOU,
SINGIN' THROUGH DE SUNSHINE,
SWEET AND CLEAR AS CAN BE:

>*(***CABLE** *crosses to face Bali Ha'i.)*

"COME TO ME,
HERE AM I,
COME TO ME!"

IF YOU TRY,
YOU'LL FIND ME
WHERE DE SKY MEETS DE SEA:
"HERE AM I,
YOUR SPECIAL ISLAND!
COME TO ME, COME TO ME!"

BALI HA'I,
BALI HA'I,
BALI HA'I.

> *(The music continues as **BLOODY MARY** finishes, facing front, arms outstretched. She nods to **CABLE**, then exits.)*

BILLIS. Of course, Lieutenant, right now that island is off limits due to the fact that the French planters have all their young women running around over there.

> *(He pauses to observe the effect of these significant words.)*

Of course, you being an officer, you could get a launch. I'd even be willing to requisition a boat for you. What do you say, Lieutenant?

> *(Singing throatily.)*

BALI HA'I
MAY CALL YOU,
ANY NIGHT, ANY DAY.
IN YOUR HEART
YOU'LL HEAR IT CALL YOU:
"COME AWAY, COME AWAY."

Hunh, Lieutenant?

> *(Pause.)*

CABLE. No.

BILLIS. *(Making a quick shift.)* I see what you mean, being off limits and all. It would take a lot of persuading to get me to go over there... But, another thing goes on over there – the ceremonial boar's tooth. After they kill the boar they pass around some of that coconut liquor and women dance with just skirts on...

(His voice becoming evil.) ...and everybody gets to know everybody pretty well...

BALI HA'I
WILL WHISPER
ON DE WIND OF DE SEA:

"HERE AM I,
YOUR SPECIAL ISLAND!
COME TO ME, COME TO ME!"

It's just a little tribal ceremonial, primitive but *as-s-tonishing*, and I thought you being up in the shooting war for such a long time without getting any... recreation – I thought you might be interested.

CABLE. I am. But right now I've got to report to the Island Commander.

BILLIS. Oh.

(Shouting officiously.) Professor! Take the Lieutenant up in the truck.

CABLE. Professor?

BILLIS. That's because he went to college. You go to college?

CABLE. Er...yes.

BILLIS. Where?

CABLE. A place in New Jersey.

BILLIS. Where? Rutgers?

CABLE. No...Princeton.

BILLIS. Oh. Folks got money, eh, Lieutenant?

> (**CABLE** *turns away,* **BILLIS** *pats him on the back.*)

Don't be ashamed of it. We understand. Say! Maybe you'd like to hear the Professor talk some language. What would you like to hear? Latin? Grecian?

> (**BILLIS** *grabs the unwilling* **PROFESSOR** *by the arm and leads him over to* **CABLE**.)

Aw, give him some Latin.

PROFESSOR. *(Feeling pretty silly, but proceeds.)* "Rectius vives Licini..."

BILLIS. Ain't that beautiful!

PROFESSOR. "...neque altum Semper urgendo dum procellas."

> *(A crowd gathers around the* **PROFESSOR**. **BILLIS** *beams at* **CABLE**.*)*

BILLIS. Now, Lieutenant, what did he say?

CABLE. I'm afraid I haven't the slightest idea.

BILLIS. What's the matter, didn't you graduate?

(Disgusted, to the **PROFESSOR.***)* Take the Lieutenant to the buildings.

*(***CABLE** *and the* **PROFESSOR** *start to exit.)*

PROFESSOR. Aye, aye!

BILLIS. *(To* **STEWPOT.***)* He'll never make Captain.

> *(The* **PROFESSOR,** *suddenly alarmed by something he sees offstage, turns back and starts to make strange signal-noises of warning.* **BLOODY MARY** *enters below her kiosk.)*

PROFESSOR. Whoop – whoop – whoop.

(In a horse whisper.) Iron Belly!

> *(The* **MEN** *assume casual and innocent attitudes. Some make bird sounds.* **BLOODY MARY** *looks off and walks back to her kiosk to stand defiantly in front of it.* **CABLE,** *puzzled, stands by to await developments. What develops is that "Iron Belly,"* **CAPTAIN BRACKETT,** *enters, followed by his executive officer,* **COMMANDER HARBISON.***)*

HARBISON. Here she is, sir.

> *(He points to* **BLOODY MARY,** *who is standing her ground doggedly in front of her kiosk.* **BRACKETT** *walks slowly over to her.* **HARBISON** *takes a few steps toward the* **MEN,** *and they move away.* **BRACKETT** *glares at* **BLOODY MARY.** *Undaunted, she glares right back.)*

BRACKETT. You are causing an economic revolution on this island. These French planters can't find a native to pick a coconut or milk a cow because you're paying them ten times as much to make these ridiculous grass skirts.

BLOODY MARY. French planters stingy bastards!

(**STEWPOT** *drops a tin bucket. The* **MEN** *control themselves from laughing by great efforts.* **BILLIS** *approaches* **BRACKETT** *with a snappy salute.*)

BILLIS. Sir! May I make a suggestion, sir?

BRACKETT. *(Returning salute.)* Who are you?

BILLIS. *(Disappointed that* **BRACKETT** *doesn't remember him.)* Billis, sir, Luther Billis.

(*Making an impressive announcement.*)

The natives can now go back to work on the farms. The demand for grass skirts can now be met by us Seabees!

BRACKETT. Dressmakers!

(*Starting to blow up.*)

Do you mean to tell me the Seabees of the United States Navy are now a lot of...

BILLIS. *(Cutting him off.)* If you don't like the idea, sir, we can drop it right here, sit. Just say the word. Just pretend I never brought it up.

HARBISON. *(Reflectively.)* Luther Billis.

BILLIS. *(With an eager salute.)* Yes, sir?

HARBISON. Nothing. Just making a mental note. I want to be sure not to forget your name.

(**BILLIS**' *salute dissolves; he slowly and dejectedly retires.*)

BRACKETT. *(Turns to* **BLOODY MARY**.*)* I want to see you pick up every scrap of this paraphernalia now! And, for the last time, carry it way down there beyond that fence off Navy property.

(**BLOODY MARY** *stands firmly planted and immovable!* **CABLE** *walks to the kiosk and collapses it.*)

CABLE. *(With decisive authority.)* Come on, everybody. Take all this stuff and throw it over that fence.

(*The* **MEN** *quickly obey,* **BILLIS** *ostentatiously taking charge in front of the two* **OFFICERS**.)

BILLIS. *(To* **MEN**, *as they exit.)* All right – take it way down there. Off Navy property!

CABLE. *(Strides over to* **BLOODY MARY** *and points off.)* You go too.

BLOODY MARY. *(***CABLE** *can do no wrong in her eyes.)* All right, Lootellan. Thank you.

> *(She exits. By this time, all the* **MEN** *have gone, taking her kiosk with them.* **BRACKETT**, **CABLE**, *and* **HARBISON** *are left.* **BRACKETT** *looks at* **HARBISON** *as if to ask who* **CABLE** *is.* **HARBISON** *shrugs his shoulders.* **CABLE** *turns and exchanges salutes with* **BRACKETT**.*)*

BRACKETT. Lieutenant, who are you, anyway?

CABLE. I'm Lieutenant Joseph Cable, sir. I just flew in on that PBY.

BRACKETT. A joyride?

CABLE. No, sir. Orders.

BRACKETT. A Marine under orders to me?

CABLE. Yes, sir.

BRACKETT. I'm Captain Brackett.

CABLE. How do you do, sir?

BRACKETT. This is Commander Harbison, my Executive Officer.

> *(***CABLE** *and* **HARBISON** *exchange salutes and handshakes.)*

Well, what's it all about?

CABLE. My Colonel feels that all these islands are in danger because none of us has been getting first-hand intelligence, and what we need is a coast watch.

HARBISON. A coast watch?

CABLE. *(Drawing a rough map in the sand.)* A man with a radio hiding out on one of those enemy-held islands, where he could watch for ships when they start down the bottleneck...down this way.

BRACKETT. *(Turning to* **HARBISON**.*)* What do you think, Bill?

HARBISON. Well, sir, our pilots could do a hell of a lot to enemy convoys with information like that.

BRACKETT. You'd have to sneak this man ashore at night from a submarine.

CABLE. Yes, sir.

HARBISON. Who's going to do it?

CABLE. Well, sir...*I've* been elected.

(Pause.)

BRACKETT. *(After exchanging a look with* **HARBISON.***)* You've got quite an assignment, son.

HARBISON. How long do you think you could last there, sending out messages, before the enemy found you?

CABLE. I think I'd be okay if I could take a man with me who really knew the country. Headquarters has found out there's a French civilian here who used to have a plantation on Marie Louise Island.

HARBISON. Marie Louise! That's a good spot. Right on the bottleneck.

BRACKETT. What's this Frenchman's name?

CABLE. Emile de Becque.

BRACKETT. *(Suddenly excited.)* Meet me in my office in about half an hour, Cable.

(He starts off, followed by **HARBISON.***)*

CABLE. Yes, sir.

BRACKETT. Come on, Bill! Maybe we'll get into this war yet!

(They exit. **CABLE** *watches them off, then picks up his bag and starts off.)*

[MUSIC NO. 16 "CABLE HEARS 'BALI HA'I'"]

*(**CABLE** stops in his tracks and listens. Then he turns and looks across at the island. Softly, he starts to sing.)*

CABLE.
BALI HA'I
MAY CALL YOU,

ANY NIGHT, ANY DAY,
IN YOUR HEART
YOU'LL HEAR IT CALL YOU:
"COME AWAY, COME AWAY!"
BALI HA'I,
BALI HA'I,
BALI HA'I.

>*(He exits.)*
>
>**[MUSIC NO. 17 "CHANGE OF SCENE (COMPANY STREET)"]**

Scene Four
The Company Street

*(As **CABLE** sings, the lights fade. Downstage, several **G.I.S** enter, carrying ammo boxes, jerry cans, and various articles of equipment. A curtain closes depicting a Company Street.)*

SAILOR. When are you guys going to get that lumber in our area?

SEABEE. *(Passing him.)* Aw, knock it off!

SAILOR. We'll never get it finished by Thanksgiving.

*(Lights up full on the Company Street. **NATIVES** and **G.I.S** are constantly crossing, carrying equipment. **NATIVES** are seen sometimes wearing bits of G.I. uniforms and sometimes just native cloths. Two **NURSES** in white uniforms cross. Then **BILLIS** enters, in earnest conversation with **STEWPOT** and the **PROFESSOR**.)*

BILLIS. Did you tell those guys at the shop to stop making those grass skirts?

STEWPOT. Sure, they just turned out one of these.

*(He hands **BILLIS** a small, dark object.)*

What do you think of it?

BILLIS. *(Studying it a moment.)* That don't look like a dried-up human head. It looks like an old orange painted with shoe polish.

STEWPOT. That's what it is.

BILLIS. Go back to the shop and tell them to try again. If I order a dried-up human head, I want a human head – dried up!

(He puts the orange in his pocket.)

STEWPOT. But...

BILLIS. Fade. Here he comes.

> (**STEWPOT** *and the* **PROFESSOR** *move away as* **CABLE** *enters.* **BILLIS** *crosses to him and speaks in a low voice, right in* **CABLE***'s ear, as he walks alongside him.*)

Don't change your expression, Lieutenant. Just act like we're talking casual. I got the boat.

CABLE. *(Stops.)* What boat?

BILLIS. Keep walking down the Company Street. Keep your voice down.

> (**CABLE** *walks slowly and uncertainly.*)

I signed out a boat in your name. We're shoving off for Bali Ha'i in forty-five minutes.

CABLE. *(Stopping.)* No, we're not. I've got to see Captain Brackett.

BILLIS. *(An injured man.)* Lieutenant! What are you doing to me? I signed this boat out in your name.

CABLE. Then you're just the man to go back and cancel it. *(Very firmly.)* Forget the whole thing. Okay?

> *(He exits.)*

BILLIS. *(To where* **CABLE** *exited.)* Lieutenant, you and me are going on a boat trip whether you like it or not.

> *(He pulls the orange, covered with shoe polish, out of his pocket, and wishing to vent his rage somehow, he turns and hurls it off in the direction opposite that taken by* **CABLE***.)*

A FURIOUS VOICE. *(Offstage.)* Hey! Who the hell threw that?

BILLIS. *(Spoiling for a fight with anyone at all.)* I threw it! What are you gonna do about it?

> *(He strides off pugnaciously in the direction of the voice. Before he is off, the curtains have parted on the succeeding scene.)*

Scene Five
Inside the Island Commander's Office

(**BRACKETT** *is sitting at his desk, reading some papers.* **HARBISON** *stands above him.* **CABLE** *sits on a chair facing the desk.*)

BRACKETT. Cable – we've got some dope on your Frenchman.

(*He reads a paper before him.*)

Marie Louise Island…moved down here sixteen years ago…lived with a Polynesian woman for about five years…two children by her. She died… Here's one thing we've got to clear up. Seems he left France in a hurry. Killed a guy. What do you think of that?

CABLE. Might be a handy man to have around.

(*The phone rings.*)

HARBISON. (*Beckoning to* **CABLE.**) Cable.

(**CABLE** *joins him and they inspect a map on the wall.*)

BRACKETT. (*On phone.*) Good – send her in. No, we haven't got time for her to change into her uniform. Tell her to come in.

(*The* **MEN** *exchange looks and face the doorway, where presently* **NELLIE** *appears.*)

Come in, Miss Forbush.

NELLIE. Captain Brackett, please excuse the way…

BRACKETT. You look fine. May I present Commander Harbison?

HARBISON. I have the pleasure of meeting Miss Forbush twice a week.

(**BRACKETT** *looks at him with surprised admiration.*)

We serve together on the G.I. Entertainment Committee.

BRACKETT. Oh. May I also present Lieutenant Joseph Cable – Miss Forbush. Sit down, Miss Forbush.

(The three MEN rush to help her sit. CABLE gets there first. NELLIE sits. BRACKETT sits on his desk facing her. CABLE drops upstage. BRACKETT starts off with light conversation.)

How's the Thanksgiving entertainment coming along?

NELLIE. Very well, thank you, sir. We practice whenever we get a chance.

(She wonders why she has been sent for.)

BRACKETT. About a week ago, you had lunch with a French planter – Emile de Becque.

NELLIE. Yes, sir.

BRACKETT. What do you know about him?

NELLIE. *(Thrown off balance.)* Well, I…er…what do I know about him?

BRACKETT. That's right.

NELLIE. I…we…met at the Officers' Club dance. He was there and I…met him.

(She stops, hoping they will help her along, but they say nothing, so she has to continue.)

Then I had lunch with him that day…

BRACKETT. *(Quickly.)* Yes! Now, what kind of a man is he?

NELLIE. He's very nice… He's kind… He's attractive. I…er… Just don't know what you want to know, sir.

HARBISON. Miss Forbush, Captain Brackett wants to know, did you discuss politics?

NELLIE. No, sir.

BRACKETT. *(After a long, pitying look at HARBISON.)* Would you have discussed politics, Commander?

(Turning back to NELLIE.)

Now, what we are specifically interested in is…er… when these fellows come out from France, it's generally because they've had some trouble.

(NELLIE looks worried.)

Now…has he ever told you anything about that?

(**NELLIE** *hesitates a moment, deliberating just how far to go in her answer.* **BRACKETT** *tries to help her out, sensing her embarrassment.*)

BRACKETT. What do you know about his family?

NELLIE. (*Glad to be able to answer a simple, specific question without incriminating Emile.*) He has no family – no wife, nobody.

HARBISON. He hasn't any children?

(**CABLE** *and* **HARBISON** *exchange looks.*)

NELLIE. No, sir!

BRACKETT. And you say he's never told you why he left France?

(*Pause. Then* **NELLIE** *answers as a Navy Ensign should.*)

NELLIE. Yes, sir. He left France because he killed a man.

(*A sigh of relief from* **BRACKETT**.)

HARBISON. Did he tell you why?

NELLIE. No. But he will if I ask him.

HARBISON. Well, Miss Forbush, that's exactly what we'd like to have you do. Find out as much as you can about him, his background, his opinions, and why he killed this man in France.

NELLIE. In other words, you want me to spy on him.

BRACKETT. Well, I'm afraid it is something like that.

NELLIE. Why?

(*Alarmed, she rises and faces* **BRACKETT** *across the desk.*)

Do you suspect him of something?

BRACKETT. (*Lies do not come easy to him.*) No, it's just that we don't know very much about him and he's...er... Will you help us, Miss Forbush?

(*Pause.*)

NELLIE. I'll try.

BRACKETT. Thank you. You may go now if you wish.

(She starts toward the door, then turns, thoughtfully, as if asking the question of herself.)

NELLIE. I don't know very much about him really...do I?

*(Slowly, she goes out. For a moment, the **MEN** are silent.)*

CABLE. He's kept a few secrets from her, hasn't he?

BRACKETT. Well, you don't spring a couple of Polynesian kids on a woman right off the bat!

HARBISON. I'm afraid we aren't going to get much out of her. She's obviously in love with him.

CABLE. *(To **HARBISON**.)* That's hard to believe, sir. They tell me he's a middle-aged man.

BRACKETT. *(Rising from his desk chair. Smoldering.)* Cable! It is a common mistake for boys of your age and athletic ability to underestimate men who have reached their maturity.

CABLE. I didn't mean, sir...

BRACKETT. Young women frequently find a grown man attractive, strange as it may seem to you. I myself am over fifty. I am a bachelor and, Cable, I do not, by any means, consider myself...through.

*(To **HARBISON**, who is suppressing laughter.)* What's the matter, Bill?

HARBISON. Nothing. Evidently!

BRACKETT. Okay, Cable. See you at chow. Do you play bridge?

CABLE. Yes, sir.

BRACKETT. Got any money?

CABLE. Yes, sir.

BRACKETT. I'll take it away from you.

CABLE. Yes, sir.

*(He goes out. **BRACKETT** darts a penetrating look at **HARBISON**.)*

BRACKETT. What makes you so *damn sure* this mission won't work out?

HARBISON. *(Looking at the map.)* Marie Louise Island is twenty-four miles long and three miles wide. Let's say that every time they send out a message they move to another hill. It seems to me, looking at this thing...

BRACKETT. Realistically.

HARBISON. ...Realistically...

> *(Measuring his words.)*

...they could last about a week.

> *(Pause. BRACKETT considers this.)*

BRACKETT. Of course, it would be worth it, if it were the right week. With decent information, our side might get moving. Operation Alligator might get off its can.

QUALE. *(Entering with a large cardboard box.)* Here it is, sir – I got it.

BRACKETT. *(To HARBISON.)* Okay, Bill. See you at chow.

> *(HARBISON looks at the package curiously.)*

See you at chow, Bill.

HARBISON. *(Snapping out of it.)* Oh, see you at chow.

> *(He goes out.)*

BRACKETT. Got the address right?

QUALE. I think so, sir.

> *(Reading the box lid.)* Mrs. Amelia Fortuna. Three twenty-five Euclid Avenue, Shaker Heights, Cleveland, Ohio.

BRACKETT. That's right. I want to pack it myself.

QUALE. Yes, sir.

> *(He exits. BRACKETT starts to whistle. He opens the package and takes out a bright-yellow grass skirt and shakes it out. HARBISON re-enters, stands in the doorway, unseen by BRACKETT, nods as if his suspicions were confirmed, and exists as the lights fade.)*

[MUSIC NO. 18 "COMPANY STREET (CONTINUATION)"]

Scene Six
The Company Street

(As lights fade on the Captain's hut, the Company Street curtain closes and the activity seen before resumes. **G.I.S** *and* **NATIVES** *cross, carrying various items of equipment.* **NELLIE** *enters, walking slowly as she reads a letter. Another* **NURSE** *in working uniform has some letters in her hand and is moving off.)*

NURSE. Going to the beach, Nellie?

*(***NELLIE** *nods. The* **NURSE** *exits.* **CABLE** *enters and watches* **NELLIE** *for a moment. She is now standing still, reading a part of a letter that evokes an occasional groan of irritation from her.* **CABLE** *grins at her.)*

CABLE. Letter from home?

*(***NELLIE** *looks up, startled by his voice, then grins back at him.)*

NELLIE. Yes. Do you get letters from your mother, telling you that everything you do is wrong?

CABLE. No. My mother thinks everything I do is right... Of course, I don't tell her everything I do.

NELLIE. My mother's so prejudiced.

CABLE. Against Frenchmen?

*(***NELLIE** *smiles to acknowledge that she gets the allusion, then pursues her anti-maternal tirade.)*

NELLIE. Against anyone outside of Little Rock. She makes a big thing out of two people having different backgrounds.

CABLE. *(Rather hopefully.)* Ages?

NELLIE. Oh, no. Mother says older men are better for girls than younger men.

CABLE. This has been a discouraging day for me.

NELLIE. Do you agree with Mother about people having things in common? For instance, if the man likes symphony music and the girl likes Dinah Shore – and he reads Marcel Proust and she doesn't read anything. Well, what do *you* think? Do you think Mother's right?

CABLE. Well, she might be.

NELLIE. Well, I don't think she is.

CABLE. Well, maybe she's not.

NELLIE. Well, good-bye, Lieutenant. You've helped a lot.

> *(She begins to exit.)*

CABLE. Listen, you don't know so much about that guy. You better read that letter over two or three times.

NELLIE. I'll show you what I think of that idea.

> *(She crumples the letter and throws it on the ground.)*

CABLE. Well, don't say I didn't warn you.

> *(He exits. **NELLIE** comes back and picks up the letter and starts reading as she walks off.)*

Scene Seven
The Beach

(The Company Street traveler opens as lights come up on the beach. Several **NURSES** *are lounging about before taking their swim. More enter. One of them,* **DINAH**, *is washing an evening dress in a tin tub. Upstage is a homemade shower bath, bearing a sign:)*

"BATH CLUB
SHOWER 15¢
USE OF SOAP 5¢
NO TOWELS SUPPLIED"

(Two or three **SEABEES** *stand in attendance, part of Billis' business empire, no doubt.)*

BILLIS. *(Entering.)* Oh, I thought Miss Forbush was here. I brought some hot water for her.

(A couple of the **NURSES** *react unbelievingly to "hot water" as* **BILLIS** *goes to the shower, climbs a ladder, and pours a bucket of water into the tank on top.)*

She likes to take a shampoo Fridays.

NELLIE. *(Entering.)* Hello, Luther.

BILLIS. Hello, Miss Forbush. I brought some hot water for you.

NELLIE. Thanks. It'll do me a lot of good to get some of this sand out of my hair.

BILLIS. If you need some extra water for rinsing your hair, my bath-club concession boys will take care of you. When you're ready for the shower, just pull this chain, just like you was...like you was pulling down a window shade. Take care of her, boys.

(He exits. **NELLIE** *enters the shower and takes off her shirt, revealing shorts and a halter top.)*

*(The **NURSES** sense something is up.)*

1ST NURSE. What'd he want?

NELLIE. Huh?

1ST NURSE. What'd he want?

NELLIE. Who?

1ST NURSE. Iron Belly.

NELLIE. Captain Brackett? Oh, nothing – nothing important. Something about the Thanksgiving show.

2ND NURSE. Then what's the trouble, Knucklehead?

NELLIE. Huh?

2ND NURSE. I said, what's the trouble?

NELLIE. Oh, nothing.

*(The **NURSES** look at one another. **NELLIE** comes out of the shower enclosure.)*

There's not going to be any trouble anymore because I've made up my mind about one thing.

(She takes a deep breath and looks at them dramatically.)

It's all off.

(She goes back into the shower.)

3RD NURSE. With him?

NELLIE. *(Coming right out again through the swinging doors.)* Unh-hunh.

(She starts back, then stops and turns.)

I'm going to break it off clean before it's too late.

4TH NURSE. Knucklehead, what's happened? What'd he do?

NELLIE. *He* didn't do anything. It's just that… Well, I guess I don't know anything about him really and before I go any further with this thing… I just better not get started! Don't you think so, too? Diney?

DINAH. Yes, I do.

NELLIE. *(Unprepared for such prompt and unequivocal agreement.)* You do? Well, I guess I do, too.

*(She turns to the other **NURSES**.)*

Well, don't look so dramatic about it. Things like this happen every day.

[MUSIC NO. 19 "I'M GONNA WASH THAT MAN RIGHT OUTA MY HAIR"]

I'M GONNA WASH THAT MAN RIGHT OUTA MY HAIR,
I'M GONNA WASH THAT MAN RIGHT OUTA MY HAIR,
I'M GONNA WASH THAT MAN RIGHT OUTA MY HAIR,
AND SEND HIM ON HIS WAY!

Get the picture?

I'M GONNA WASH THAT MAN RIGHT OUTA MY ARMS,
I'M GONNA WASH THAT MAN RIGHT OUTA MY ARMS,
I'M GONNA WASH THAT MAN RIGHT OUTA MY ARMS,
AND SEND HIM ON HIS WAY!

DON'T TRY TO PATCH IT UP –

NURSES.
TEAR IT UP, TEAR IT UP!

NELLIE.
WASH HIM OUT, DRY HIM OUT,

NURSES.
PUSH HIM OUT, FLY HIM OUT,

NELLIE.
CANCEL HIM AND LET HIM GO!

NURSES.
YEA, SISTER!
I'M GONNA WASH THAT MAN RIGHT OUTA MY HAIR,
I'M GONNA WASH THAT MAN RIGHT OUTA MY HAIR,
I'M GONNA WASH THAT MAN RIGHT OUTA MY HAIR,
AND SEND HIM ON HIS WAY!

NELLIE.
IF THE MAN DON'T UNDERSTAND YOU,
IF YOU FLY ON SEPARATE BEAMS,
WASTE NO TIME! MAKE A CHANGE,
RIDE THAT MAN RIGHT OFF YOUR RANGE,
RUB HIM OUTA THE ROLL CALL
AND DRUM HIM OUTA YOUR DREAMS!

NURSES.
> OH – HO!

DINAH.
> IF YOU LAUGH AT DIFFERENT COMICS,

JANET.
> IF YOU ROOT FOR DIFFERENT TEAMS,

NELLIE, DINAH & JANET.
> WASTE NO TIME,
> WEEP NO MORE,
> SHOW HIM WHAT THE DOOR IS FOR!

NURSES.
> RUB HIM OUTA THE ROLL CALL
> AND DRUM HIM OUTA YOUR DREAMS!

NELLIE.
> YOU CAN'T LIGHT A FIRE WHEN THE WOOD'S ALL WET!

NURSES. No!

NELLIE.
> YOU CAN'T MAKE A BUTTERFLY STRONG.

NURSES. Uh-uh!

NELLIE.
> YOU CAN'T FIX AN EGG WHEN IT AIN'T QUITE GOOD,

NURSES.
> AND YOU CAN'T FIX A MAN WHEN HE'S WRONG!

NELLIE.
> YOU CAN'T PUT BACK A PETAL
> WHEN IT FALLS FROM A FLOWER,
> OR SWEETEN UP A FELLER
> WHEN HE STARTS TURNING SOUR –

(She goes back into the shower.)

NURSES.
> OH, NO! OH, NO!

*(Music continues. **NELLIE** turns the water on, wets her hair, and lathers up. She comes out fully soaped and struts about, splashing the **NURSES** with suds. Everyone has a silly time of it before **NELLIE** returns to the shower and rinses her hair as the **NURSES** sing.)*

IF HIS EYES GET DULL AND FISHY
WHEN YOU LOOK FOR GLINTS AND GLEAMS,
WASTE NO TIME,
MAKE A SWITCH,
DROP HIM IN THE NEAREST DITCH!
RUB HIM OUTA THE ROLL CALL
AND DRUM HIM OUTA YOUR DREAMS!
OH - HO! OH - HO!

> *(There is silence as **NELLIE** pokes her head out from the shower. She is handed a towel, wipes her face, looks up, and sings.)*

NELLIE.
I WENT AN' WASHED THAT MAN RIGHT OUTA MY HAIR,
I WENT AN' WASHED THAT MAN RIGHT OUTA MY HAIR,
I WENT AN' WASHED THAT MAN RIGHT OUTA MY HAIR,
AND SENT HIM ON HIS WAY!

NURSES. *(Each line quieter than the one before.)*
SHE WENT AN' WASHED THAT MAN RIGHT OUTA HER HAIR,
SHE WENT AN' WASHED THAT MAN RIGHT OUTA HER HAIR,
SHE WENT AN' WASHED THAT MAN RIGHT OUTA HER HAIR,

ALL. *(Forte in a triumphant finish.)*
AND SENT HIM ON HIS WAY!

> *(**NELLIE** continues to dry her hair with the towel. **EMILE** enters; **NELLIE** cannot see him, but the rest of the **NURSES** can. They quickly slip away, all but **DINAH**.)*

[MUSIC NO. 20 "I'M GONNA WASH THAT MAN... (NELLIE'S ENCORE)"]

> *(**NELLIE** partly sings, partly hums the song as she dries her hair, towel still over her head. Suddenly she stops – she has seen something on the ground: **EMILE**'s shoes. She moves closes to them, holding the towel forward as a photographer holds their cloth. She scurries*

>*over to **DINAH** for confirmation, still holding the towel. **DINAH** nods as if to say: "That's him, all right." **NELLIE** makes a dash for the shower. While she is putting a top-piece on over her halter top, **DINAH** goes to her tin tub to take out her evening dress. She stands in front of the shower, blocking the way, trying to make conversation with **EMILE**. She looks and feels very silly.)*

DINAH. *(Stalling for time.)* You'd never think this was an evening dress would you? We're only allowed to bring two of them – evening dresses...only two... I brought...

>*(She retreats offstage, with no grace whatever. **NELLIE** comes out of the shower and makes a naïve attempt to appear surprised.)*

NELLIE. Hello!

EMILE. Hello. That song – is it a new American song?

NELLIE. It's an American-type song. We were kind of putting in our own words.

>*(Looking around.)*

Where is everybody?

EMILE. It is strange with your American songs. In all of them one is either desirous to get rid of one's lover, or one weeps for a man one cannot have.

NELLIE. That's right.

EMILE. I like a song that says: "I love you and you love me... And isn't that fine?"

NELLIE. *(Not very bright at the moment.)* Yes...that's fine.

EMILE. I left a note for you at the hospital. It was to ask you to my home for dinner next Friday.

NELLIE. Well, I don't think I'll be able to come, Emile, I...

EMILE. I have asked all my friends. The planters' colony.

NELLIE. *(Determined to wash him out of her hair.)* Oh, a big party. Well, then, if I can't come, you won't miss me.

EMILE. But it *is for* you. It is for my friends to meet you and – more important – for you to meet them; to give you an idea of what your life would be like here. I want you to know more about me – how I live and think.

NELLIE. *(Suddenly remembering her promise to "spy on him.")* Know more about you?

EMILE. Yes. You know very little about me.

NELLIE. That's right!

(Getting down to business.)

Would you sit down?

*(**EMILE** sits. **NELLIE** paces like a cross-examiner.)*

Do you think about politics much... And if so, what do you think about politics?

EMILE. Do you mean my political philosophy?

NELLIE. I think that's what I mean.

EMILE. Well, to begin with, I believe in the free life – in freedom for everyone.

NELLIE. *(Eagerly.)* Like in the Declaration of Independence?

EMILE. C'est ça. All men are created equal, isn't it?

NELLIE. Emile! You really believe that?

EMILE. Yes.

NELLIE. *(With great relief.)* Well, thank goodness!

EMILE. It is why I am here – why I killed a man.

NELLIE. *(Brought back to her mission.)* Oh, yes. I meant to ask you about that too. I don't want you to think I'm prying into your private life, asking a lot of questions. But...I always think it's interesting why a person...kills another person.

*(**EMILE** smile understandingly.)*

EMILE. Of course, Nellie. That has worried you.

(He turns away to gather his thoughts.)

When I was a boy, I carried my heart in my hand...so... when this man came to our town – though my father said he was good – I thought he was bad.

EMILE. *(With a shrug and a smile.)* I was young... He attracted all the mean and cruel people to him. Soon he was running our town! He could do anything – take anything – I did not like that. I was young. I stood up in the public square and made a speech. I called upon everyone to stand with me against this man.

NELLIE. What did they do?

EMILE. *(Letting his hands fall helplessly to his sides.)* They walked away!

NELLIE. Why?

EMILE. Because they saw him standing behind me. I turned, and he said to me, "I am going to kill you now." We fought. I was never so strong. I knocked him to the ground. And when he fell, his head struck a stone and...

> *(He turns away and lets **NELLIE** imagine the rest.)*

I ran to the waterfront and joined a cargo boat. I didn't even know where it was going. I stepped off that boat into another world –

> *(He looks around him, loving all he sees.)*

– where I am now...and where I want to stay.

[MUSIC NO. 21 "INTRO TO 'SOME ENCHANTED EVENING (REPRISE)'"]

> *(He turns to **NELLIE** and impulsively steps toward her, deep sincerity and anxiety in his voice.)*

Nellie, will you marry me? There are so few days in our life, Nellie. The time I have with you now is precious to me...

Have you been thinking?

NELLIE. I have been thinking.
>   BORN ON THE OPPOSITE SIDES OF A SEA,
>   WE ARE AS DIFFERENT AS PEOPLE CAN BE.

EMILE.
>   IT'S TRUE.

NELLIE.
>AND YET YOU WANT TO MARRY ME.

EMILE.
>I DO.

NELLIE.
>I'VE KNOWN YOU A FEW SHORT WEEKS AND YET
>SOMEHOW YOU'VE MADE MY HEART FORGET
>ALL OTHER MEN I HAVE EVER MET
>BUT YOU... BUT YOU...

[MUSIC NO. 22 "SOME ENCHANTED EVENING (REPRISE)"]

EMILE.
>SOME ENCHANTED EVENING
>YOU MAY SEE A STRANGER
>YOU MAY SEE A STRANGER
>ACROSS A CROWDED ROOM.
>AND SOMEHOW YOU KNOW,
>YOU KNOW EVEN THEN,
>THAT SOMEWHERE YOU'LL SEE HER
>AGAIN AND AGAIN.

NELLIE.
>WHO CAN EXPLAIN IT?
>WHO CAN TELL YOU WHY?

EMILE.
>FOOLS GIVE YOU REASONS –
>WISE MEN NEVER TRY.
>
>SOME ENCHANTED EVENING,
>WHEN YOU FIND YOUR TRUE LOVE,
>WHEN YOU FEEL HER CALL YOU
>ACROSS A CROWDED ROOM –
>THEN FLY TO HER SIDE
>AND MAKE HER YOUR OWN,
>OR ALL THROUGH YOUR LIFE YOU MAY DREAM ALL ALONE.

NELLIE. *(Clinging to him.)*
>ONCE YOU HAVE FOUND HER,
>NEVER LET HER GO.

EMILE.
> ONCE YOU HAVE FOUND HER,
> NEVER LET HER GO!

> *(They kiss.)*

> **[MUSIC NO. 23 "INTRO TO 'I'M IN LOVE WITH A WONDERFUL GUY'"]**

Will you come next Friday?

NELLIE. *(Somewhere, from out of the ether, she hears her voice murmur an inarticulate but automatic assent.)* Uh-huh.

> *(**EMILE** kisses her again and leaves. There is the sound of laughter offstage right and a voice is heard.)*

NURSE. *(Offstage.)* Well, she sure washed him out of her hair!

> *(General laughter from the **NURSES** offstage right and left.)*

ANOTHER NURSE. *(Offstage, loudly.)* Quiet – she'll hear you.

> **[MUSIC NO. 24 "I'M IN LOVE WITH A WONDERFUL GUY"]**

> *(**NELLIE** looks defiantly off in the direction of her mocking friends and sings the verse as much to them as possible.)*

NELLIE.
> I EXPECT EVERY ONE
> OF MY CROWD TO MAKE FUN
> OF MY PROUD PROTESTATIONS OF FAITH IN ROMANCE,

> *(Sound of laughter. **NELLIE** crosses right and defiantly sings at offstage **NURSES**.)*

> AND THEY'LL SAY I'M NAÏVE
> AS A BABE TO BELIEVE
> ANY FABLE I HEAR FROM A PERSON IN PANTS.

> *(Sound of laughter off left brings **NELLIE** back to center as she sings out front.)*

FEARLESSLY I'LL FACE THEM AND ARGUE THEIR DOUBTS AWAY.
LOUDLY I'LL SING ABOUT FLOWERS AND SPRING.
FLATLY I'LL STAND ON MY LITTLE FLAT FEET AND SAY,
"LOVE IS A GRAND AND A BEAUTIFUL THING!"
I'M NOT ASHAMED TO REVEAL
THE WORLD-FAMOUS FEELING I FEEL.

> *(She comes downstage and sits on a wooden box. She pulls back a bit, as if controlling her real feelings, and sings the chorus directly out front.)*

I'M AS CORNY AS KANSAS IN AUGUST,
I'M AS NORMAL AS BLUEBERRY PIE.
NO MORE A SMART LITTLE GIRL WITH NO HEART,
I HAVE FOUND ME A WONDERFUL GUY.
I AM IN A CONVENTIONAL DITHER
WITH A CONVENTIONAL STAR IN MY EYE,
AND YOU WILL NOTE THERE'S A LUMP IN MY THROAT
WHEN I SPEAK OF THAT WONDERFUL GUY.

I'M AS TRITE AND AS GAY
AS A DAISY IN MAY,
A CLICHÉ COMING TRUE!
I'M BROMIDIC AND BRIGHT
AS A MOON-HAPPY NIGHT
POURING LIGHT ON THE DEW.

I'M AS CORNY AS KANSAS IN AUGUST,
HIGH AS A FLAG ON THE FOURTH OF JULY!
IF YOU'LL EXCUSE AN EXPRESSION I USE,
I'M IN LOVE, I'M IN LOVE, I'M IN LOVE, I'M IN LOVE,

> *(She can hold back her feelings no longer as she rises in preparation for her dance.)*

I'M IN LOVE WITH A WONDERFUL GUY!

> *(Without taking the applause, the music continues and **NELLIE** begins a simple, joyous dance around the stage, alone. She spots*

Emile's hat, which he has left behind, hugs it, and dances with it. She does a waltz-clog around an upturned rowboat with the hat pulled down over her face. Then she jumps up on the boat and sings.)

NELLIE.

I'M AS CORNY AS KANSAS IN AUGUST,
HIGH AS A FLAG ON THE FOURTH OF JULY!

*(The other **NURSES** enter, doing imitations of a love-sick **NELLIE**.)*

IF YOU'LL EXCUSE AN EXPRESSION I USE,
I'M IN LOVE, I'M IN LOVE, I'M IN LOVE,
I'M IN LOVE, I'M IN LOVE WITH A WONDERFUL

1ST NURSE.

I'M IN LOVE,

2ND NURSE.

I'M IN LOVE,

3 MORE NURSES.

I'M IN LOVE,

NURSES.

I'M IN LOVE I'M IN LOVE WITH A WONDERFUL

NELLIE.

I'M IN

NELLIE & NURSES.

LOVE, I'M IN LOVE, I'M LOVE, I'M IN LOVE,
I'M IN LOVE WITH A WONDERFUL GUY!

(After applause, music continues.)

Scene Eight
The Company Street

[MUSIC NO. 25 "I'M IN LOVE WITH A WONDERFUL GUY (ENCORE)"]

(The Company Street traveler closes. As the lights come up, the **MEN** *are seen pursuing the activities which have characterized previous Company Street scenes. The* **NURSES** *re-enter on the Company Street, reprising the song, with* **NELLIE** *running on last and finishing in a triumphant coda to the amusement of the* **G.I.S.***)*

NURSES.

I'M AS CORNY AS KANSAS IN AUGUST,
HIGH AS A FLAG ON THE FOURTH OF JULY!
IF YOU'LL EXCUSE AN EXPRESSION I USE,

NELLIE & NURSES. *(Alternating.)*

I'M IN LOVE, I'M IN LOVE, I'M IN LOVE, I'M IN LOVE,
I'M IN LOVE, I'M IN LOVE, I'M IN LOVE, I'M IN LOVE,
I'M IN LOVE, I'M IN LOVE, I'M IN LOVE, I'M IN LOVE,
I'M IN LOVE WITH A WONDERFUL GUY!!

[MUSIC NO. 26 "INTRO TO SCENE NINE"]

Scene Nine
Inside the Island Commander's Office

(The Company Street traveler is opened to reveal Brackett's office once again. **BRACKETT**, **HARBISON**, *and* **CABLE** *are all looking intently at* **EMILE**.*)*

BRACKETT. Now, before you give us your answer, I want to impress you with three things. First, you are a civilian and you don't have to go. There's no way of our making you go. Second, this is a very dangerous mission and there's no guarantee that you'll survive – or that it will do any good. Third, that it might do a great good. It might be the means of turning the tide of war in this area.

EMILE. I understand all these things.

BRACKETT. Are you ready to give us your answer?

EMILE. Yes, I am.

(Pause.)

My answer must be no.

*(***CABLE**'s *foot comes down from the top of the wastebasket on which it was resting.* **HARBISON** *uncrosses his arms.* **BRACKETT** *and* **HARBISON** *exchange looks.)*

When a man faces death, he must weigh values very carefully. He must weigh the sweetness of his life against the thing he is asked to die for. The probability of death is very great – for both of us. I know that island well, Lieutenant Cable. I am not certain that I believe that what you ask me to do is...is...

BRACKETT. We're asking you to help us lick the Japanese. It's as simple as that. We're against the Japanese.

EMILE. I know what you're against. What are you for?

(He waits for an answer. They have none.)

When I was twenty-two, I thought the world hated bullies as much as I did. I was foolish – I killed one.

And I was forced to flee to an island. Since then, I have asked no help from anyone or any country. I have seen these bullies multiply and grow strong. The world sat by and watched.

CABLE. Aw, to hell with this, de Becque, let's be honest! Aren't you just a guy in love with a girl and you're putting her above everything else in the world?

(EMILE looks at CABLE for a moment before answering.)

EMILE. Yes, I do care about my life with her more than anything else in the world. It is the only thing that is important to me. This I believe in. This I am sure of. This I have. I cannot risk to lose it. Good day, gentlemen.

(He goes out. Pause. All three MEN have been rocked off their balance.)

HARBISON. *(Thoughtfully.)* He's an honest man, but he's wrong. Of course, we can't guarantee him a better world if we win. Point is, we can be damned sure it'll be worse if we lose. Can't we?

(BRACKETT and CABLE remain silent.)

(Hotly.) Well, can't we?

BRACKETT. *(Rising.)* Of course. Cable, there's a bottle of Scotch in my bottom drawer. See you tomorrow.

(He exits quickly. HARBISON goes to the desk and takes out the bottle from a drawer.)

HARBISON. This is the one he means.

(He takes two glasses and starts to pour the Scotch. QUALE enters, holding a sheaf of papers to be signed.)

QUALE. *(Querulously.)* Commander Harbison! The Old Man walked right out on me with all these orders to be signed! And there's another delegation of French planters here, complaining about that stolen pig – the one the Seabees took and barbecued. And Commander Hutton's here...

HARBISON. *(Grabbing the papers from him, irritably.)* Okay, okay! ...I'll take care of it!

QUALE. Well, all right, sir!

(He exits.)

CABLE. *(As he takes his glass of Scotch.)* What should I do, Commander Harbison? Go back to my outfit tonight?

HARBISON. *(With a drink in his hand.)* No, take a couple of days off and unwind.

CABLE. Unwind?

HARBISON. Sure. Take a boat. Go fishing.

CABLE. *(A light dawning on him, a memory of Billis' offer and Bloody Mary's song about Bali Ha'i.)* Boat!

Scene Ten
Another Part of the Island

[MUSIC NO. 27 "BALI HA'I (REPRISE)"]

(**CABLE** *puts his glass down and exits suddenly.* **HARBISON** *takes a swallow of Scotch and looks around for* **CABLE**, *who has disappeared.* **HARBISON** *rubs his face and starts to go to work as the lights fade. As the office recedes upstage, a curtain closes and a group of* **FRENCH GIRLS** *and a group of* **NATIVE GIRLS** *enter. The* **NATIVE GIRLS** *try to sell the fruits and flowers they carry in their hats to the* **FRENCH GIRLS**.)

GIRLS.
BALI HA'I
T'APPELLE,

(*A ship's bell rings offstage. A* **NATIVE KID** *enters, shouting excitedly: "Boat! Boat! Boat!"*)

DANS LE JOUR,
DANS LA NUIT,
DANS TON COEUR
TOUJOURS RÉSONNE,
"PAR ICI,
ME VOICI."

(**BILLIS**, **CABLE**, *and* **BLOODY MARY** *enter.* **BLOODY MARY** *whispers into the* **KID**'s *ear and sends him running off. The dialogue between* **CABLE**, **BILLIS**, *and* **BLOODY MARY** *is delivered simultaneously over the remainder of the* **GIRLS**' *"Bali Ha'i."*)

SI TU VEUX
TÙ M'TROUVERAS
OU LE CIEL
TROUVE LA MER.
ME VOICI,

LAISSE-MOI TE PRENDRE,
"PAR ICI,
ME VOICI."
BALI HA'I
BALI HA'I
BALI HA'I.

CABLE. Look, Billis, I didn't come over here to Bali Ha'i to see anybody cut any boar's teeth out.

BILLIS. It ain't the cutting of the boar's teeth exactly. It's what comes afterwards.

> (**CABLE** *crosses amongst the* **FRENCH GIRLS**. **BLOODY MARY**, *smiling, understands perfectly.*)

BLOODY MARY. I take you with me. Come, Lootellan. You have a good time.

(Calling to a **NATIVE**.*)* Marcel! Come here! Billis, Marcel take you to boar ceremony. Lootellan come later.

> (*Two* **FRENCH GIRLS** *have caught* **CABLE**'s *eye, and he has made up his mind to approach them when he is thwarted by two* **NUNS** *approaching the* **GIRLS**. *This makes* **CABLE** *more receptive to* **BLOODY MARY**.)

Lootellan, come with me. You have good time. Come!

> (*She leads him off as the lights fade.*)

Scene Eleven
Inside a Native Hut on Bali Ha'i

(The tabs open on the last word of the final line of "Bali Ha'i" to reveal the interior of a simple yet beautiful native hut. **BLOODY MARY** *enters, bending low to get through the doorway.* **CABLE** *follows, finding himself in the darkness, blinking.)*

CABLE. What's this?

BLOODY MARY. You wait.

CABLE. There's nobody around here.

BLOODY MARY. You wait, Lootellan.

CABLE. What's going on, Mary? What...

(A small figure appears in the doorway, a **GIRL**, *perhaps seventeen. Her black hair is drawn smooth over her head. Like* **BLOODY MARY**, *she wears a white blouse and black trousers. Barefooted she stands, silent, shy, and motionless against the wattled wall, looking at* **CABLE** *with the honest curiosity and admiration of a child. She is* **LIAT**.)

BLOODY MARY. *(To* **CABLE**, *with a sly smile.)* You like?

CABLE. *(Never taking his eyes from* **LIAT**.) Who is she?

BLOODY MARY. Liat.

LIAT. *(Nodding her head and repeating in a small voice.)* Liat.

BLOODY MARY. Is French name.

CABLE. *(Still stunned, gazing at* **LIAT**.) Liat.

BLOODY MARY. But she no French girl. She Tonkinese like me. We are ver' pretty people, no?

(She goes closer to **CABLE** *and looks at him. She turns to* **LIAT** *and then to* **CABLE**. **CABLE** *and* **LIAT** *continue to regard each other with silent, longing interest.)*

CABLE. *(Over **BLOODY MARY**'s head, to **LIAT**.)* Do you speak English?

BLOODY MARY. Only a few word. She talk French.

*(To **LIAT**.)* Français!

LIAT. Je parle Français – un peu.

> *(She holds her forefinger and thumb close together to show how very little she speaks.)*

CABLE. *(Grinning, nearly as shy as she.)* Moi, aussi – un peu.

> *(He gestures as she did. They both laugh. **BLOODY MARY** seems to have been forgotten by them both. She looks from one to the other, then with the air of one who has accomplished her purpose, she waddles to the doorway. As she exits, she lets the bamboo curtain roll down across the opening, reducing the light in the hut. There is a long moment of silence.)*

Are you afraid of me?

> *(**LIAT** looks puzzled. **CABLE** remembers she speaks no English.)*

Oh…er…avez-vous peur?

LIAT. *(Her young face serious.)* Non.

[MUSIC NO. 28 "YOUNGER THAN SPRINGTIME"]

Oui!

> *(**CABLE** takes a step toward her. She backs closer to the wall.)*

…Non.

> *(**CABLE** stops and looks at her, worried and hurt. This sign of gentleness wins her. She smiles.)*

> *(Now it is she who walks toward him. The music builds in a rapturous upsurge. **CABLE** gathers **LIAT** in his arms, she reaches her small*

arms up to his neck. He lifts her off her feet. The lights fade slowly as his hand slides her blouse up her back. The lights dim to complete darkness. Light projections of large and lovely Oriental blossoms are thrown against the drop. **NATIVE COUPLES** *stroll across the stage, only dimly seen. The music mounts ecstatically, then diminishes. The stage is clear. The light comes up on the hut again, and moonlight now comes through the opened doorway where* **CABLE** *stands. He has no shirt on.* **LIAT** *is seated on the floor, gazing up at him silently; her hair hangs loose down her back.* **CABLE** *smiles down at her.*)

CABLE. *(Trying to puzzle something out in his mind.)* But you're just a kid… How did that Bloody Mary get a kid like you to come here and… I don't get it.

> *(Suddenly realizing that she has not understood.)*

Cette vielle femme…votre amie?

LIAT. Ma mère.

CABLE. *(Horrified.)* Your mother! Bloody Mary is your mother! But she didn't tell me.

> *(***LIAT***, to divert him, suddenly throws herself in his lap; they kiss. The sound of the ship's bell is heard in the distance. They sit up.* **LIAT** *looks panic-stricken.)*

LIAT. Non, non!

> *(She covers* **CABLE***'s ears with her hands.)*

CABLE. *(Looking off.)* It's the boat all right.

> *(He turns to her, sees her little face below his, her eyes pleading with him to stay.)*

Aw, let them wait.

I TOUCH YOUR HAND
AND MY ARMS GROW STRONG,

LIKE A PAIR OF BIRDS
THAT BURST WITH SONG.
MY EYES LOOK DOWN
AT YOUR LOVELY FACE,
AND I HOLD THE WORLD
IN MY EMBRACE.

YOUNGER THAN SPRINGTIME ARE YOU,
SOFTER THAN STARLIGHT ARE YOU,
WARMER THAN WINDS OF JUNE
ARE THE GENTLE LIPS YOU GAVE ME.

GAYER THAN LAUGHTER ARE YOU,
SWEETER THAN MUSIC ARE YOU,
ANGEL AND LOVER, HEAVEN AND EARTH ARE YOU TO ME.

AND WHEN YOUR YOUTH AND JOY INVADE MY ARMS
AND FILL MY HEART AS NOW THEY DO...
THEN...

YOUNGER THAN SPRINGTIME AM I,
GAYER THAN LAUGHTER AM I,
ANGEL AND LOVER, HEAVEN AND EARTH AM I WITH YOU.

> *(The ship's bell is heard again. **CABLE** releases **LIAT**, goes to the door, looks off, comes back to her. He stoops to pick up his shirt. She tries to get it first. Each has hold of one end of it. He looks down at her and repeats, softly:)*

AND WHEN YOUR YOUTH AND JOY INVADE MY ARMS
AND FILL MY HEART AS NOW THEY DO...
THEN...
YOUNGER THAN SPRINGTIME AM I,
GAYER THAN LAUGHTER AM I
ANGEL AND LOVER, HEAVEN AND EARTH AM I WITH YOU.

> *(The music continues as he starts off. **LIAT** clings to the end of the shirt for a moment, then lets it slide through her fingers and watches **CABLE** go through the door. She sinks to her knees. The lights fade. In front of the tapa-cloth curtain, **NATIVE GIRLS** bearing*

trays of tropical flowers and **FRENCH GIRLS** *are gathered in several groups, singing traditional farewell songs to the departing crafts.)*

Scene Twelve
Near the Beach on Bali Ha'i

FRENCH GIRLS.
BALI HA'I
T'APPELLE
DANS LE JOUR
DANS LA NUIT,
DANS TON COEUR
TOUJOURS RESONNE
"PAR ICI
ME VOICI."

> *(They continue humming melody under the next few lines, then resume singing softly.* **BLOODY MARY** *and* **BILLIS** *enter in front of the curtain. They are looking off, anxiously awaiting* **CABLE**. **BILLIS** *drinks from a coconut. Its contents are responsible for his slightly drunken behavior.)*

BILLIS. *(Shouting off.)* Ring the bell again! Ring the bell again!

> *(Taking a lei from a* **FLOWER-SELLER**.*)*

I'll have another one of those.

BLOODY MARY. He come. He come. He be here soon. Don't worry, Billis.

BILLIS. Hey, Mary – please ask those boar's-tooth ceremonial fellows not to be sore at me. I didn't think those girls would do a religious dance with only skirts on. If somebody had told me it was a religious dance, I wouldn't have gotten up and danced with them.
(Looking off.) Oh! Here he comes! Here he comes.

> *(He exits.* **CABLE** *crosses in a kind of dream.* **BLOODY MARY** *smiles, ecstatic, as she sees his face. Several* **GIRLS** *try to flirt, but he is impervious to their advances and goes right by them.* **BLOODY MARY** *walks past them*

proudly and triumphantly. The **GIRLS** *throw flowers after* **BILLIS** *and* **CABLE** *with cries of "Au revoir" and laughter over the singing.)*

BLOODY MARY. *(Throwing flower garlands and shouting to the others as the* **FRENCH GIRLS** *sing the final three lines of "Bali Ha'i.")* Is gonna be my son-in-law!
(Calling off.) Goo'bye! Come back soon, Lootellan! Bali Ha'i! Come back soon!

FRENCH GIRLS.
SI TU VEUX
TU M'TROUVERAS
OU LE CIEL
TROUVE LA MER
ME VOICI
LAISSE MOI TE PRENDRE,
"PAR ICI
ME VOICI."
BALI HA'I,
BALI HA'I,
BALI HA'I.

(Lights fade as we hear the "Au revoirs" from **EMILE'S GUESTS** *leaving the party overlap with the* **FRENCH GIRLS'** *final "Bali Ha'i," and the traveler opens to reveal:)*

Scene Thirteen
Emile's Terrace

(Emile's terrace. The **GUESTS** *are leaving a party at Emile's house – we never actually see them. The good-byes continue through the darkness, all in French.* **HENRY** *enters with another* **SERVANT**. *They start to clear glasses, champagne bottles, and other leftovers of a festive party which clutter the scene.)*

GUESTS. *(Offstage.)* Bali Ha'i... Bon soir! ...Merci, Emile... Merci, mille fois!

EMILE. *(Entering upstage left and addressing* **HENRY**.*)* Pas maintenant... Demain!

GUEST. *(Offstage.)* Abientôt! Bali Ha'i.

*(***HENRY** *and the* **SERVANT** *exit.)*

Quelle charmante soiree.

NELLIE. *(Offstage.)* Good night, everybody... Good night.

MALE GUEST. *(Offstage.)* Non, non, Nellie – en Français, en Français.

NELLIE. *(Offstage, laboring with her French.)* Je...suis... enchantée...de faire...votre...connaissance!

*(***EMILE** *looks off, smiles with pride and amusement, then exits.* **GUESTS** *shout, "Bravo!" "Formidable!")*

MALE GUEST. *(Offstage.)* Bon soir, de Becque.
FEMALE GUEST. *(Offstage.)* Merci mille fois!!!

(There is the sound of a motor starting loud, then growing fainter. **EMILE** *and* **NELLIE** *enter and turn back to wave good-bye to the last guests. Then* **NELLIE** *turns to* **EMILE**, *who has been gently urging her farther into the garden. There is excitement in her voice and she speaks very rapidly.)*

NELLIE. Emile, you know I can't stay. And I've got to get that jeep back. I stole it. Or rather, I borrowed it. Or rather a fellow stole it for me. A wonderful man named Billis. I'll have to sneak around behind the hospital as it is.

EMILE. In that case, I forbid you to go! If you have to sneak back without anyone seeing you, you might just as well sneak back later.

*(**NELLIE** thinks for a moment, then comes to a quick decision.)*

NELLIE. *(Taking off her cape.)* You're absolutely right!

*(She looks guiltily at **EMILE** and screams with laughter. So does he. She puts the cape on the back of a chair.)*

I never had such a wonderful time in my whole life. All these lovely people and that cute old man who spoke French with me and made believe he understood me. And that exciting native couple who danced for us. Oh, it's so different from *Little Rock*!

(She screams the last line exuberantly, as if she hopes Little Rock would hear.)

[MUSIC NO. 29 "I'M IN LOVE WITH A WONDERFUL GUY (REPRISE)"]

*(**EMILE** laughs uproariously. **NELLIE** suddenly becomes quiet.)*

What on earth are you laughing at? Am I drunk?

EMILE. Oh, no.

NELLIE. Yes, I am. But it isn't the champagne – it's because…

I'M IN LOVE WITH A WONDERFUL GUY!
I AM IN A CONVENTIONAL DITHER
WITH A CONVENTIONAL STAR IN MY EYE
AND YOU WILL NOTE THERE'S A LUMP IN MY THROAT
WHEN I SPEAK OF THAT WONDERFUL GUY

I'M AS TRITE AND AS GAY
AS A DAISY IN MAY,

A CLICHÉ COMING TRUE!
I'M BROMIDIC AND BRIGHT
AS A MOON-HAPPY NIGHT
POURING LIGHT ON THE DEW!

> *(They go into an old-fashioned waltz, all around the stage.)*

I'M IN LOVE, I'M IN LOVE, I'M IN LOVE, I'M IN LOVE,
I'M IN LOVE WITH A WON–

EMILE.
I'M IN LOVE, I'M IN LOVE,
AND THE GIRL THAT I LOVE,
SHE THINKS I'M A WONDERFUL GUY.

> *(They stop, exhausted and laughing.* **NELLIE** *turns and picks up a half-filled glass of champagne that has been left by one of the guests.)*

NELLIE. Imagine leaving all this wonderful champagne!

> *(She drinks, then takes another glass and hands it to* **EMILE.***)*

Here, Emile! You have some, too. It's such a waste!

EMILE. Here – here's another bottle.

[MUSIC NO. 30 "THIS IS HOW IT FEELS"]

> *(He goes over to a long table that is under the windows on the porch. There are several buckets of champagne there. He takes one and fills two clean glasses and brings them to* **NELLIE.** *Meanwhile, she leans back, stretching her arms behind her head. Dreamily, she sings.)*

NELLIE.
THIS IS HOW IT FEELS,
LIVING ON A HILLSIDE…

> *(She speaks as the melody continues.)*

Here we are just like two old married people. Our guests have gone home and we're alone.

EMILE. *(Handing her the glass of champagne.)*
>THIS IS WHAT I NEED,
>THIS IS WHAT I'VE LONGED FOR,
>SOMEONE YOUNG AND SMILING,
>HERE UPON MY HILL –

>*(The music changes to "A Cockeyed Optimist.")*

NELLIE. *(She has been thinking.)* Emile, you know, my mother says we have nothing in common. But she's wrong. We have something very important in common – very much in common.

EMILE. Yes, we're both in love.

NELLIE. Yes, but more than that. We're...we're the same kind of people fundamentally – you and me. We appreciate things! We get enthusiastic about things. It's really quite exciting when two people are like that. We're not blasé. You know what I mean?

EMILE. We're both knuckleheads, cockeyed optimists.

>*(They both laugh.)*

NELLIE.
>I HEAR THE HUMAN RACE
>IS FALLING ON ITS FACE

EMILE.
>AND HASN'T VERY FAR TO GO!

NELLIE.
>BUT EVERY WHIPPORWILL
>IS SELLING ME A BILL
>AND TELLING ME IT JUST AIN'T SO.

NELLIE & EMILE.
>I COULD SAY LIFE IS JUST A BOWL OF JELLO
>AND APPEAR MORE INTELLIGENT AND SMART,
>BUT I'M STUCK,
>(LIKE A DOPE)
>WITH A THING CALLED HOPE,
>AND I CAN'T GET IT OUT OF MY HEART...
>NOT THIS HEART!

*(They smile in each other's eyes. **EMILE** suddenly gets an idea and rises.)*

EMILE. Nellie, I have a surprise for you. You sit over there – something that I have been preparing for two days. Close your eyes. No peeking.

*(He looks around for a prop, sees Nellie's cape, and takes it. He makes **NELLIE** sit by the fountain – she is mystified, but excited, like a child waiting for a surprise. **EMILE** throws the cape over his head to simulate a towel.)*

[MUSIC NO. 31 "I'M GONNA WASH THAT MAN… (ENCORE)"]

I'M GONNA WASH THAT MAN RIGHT OUTA MY HAIR,
I'M GONNA WASH THAT MAN RIGHT OUTA MY HAIR,

NELLIE. Oh, no! No!

(She writhes with embarrassment and laughter as he continues.)

EMILE.

I'M GONNA WASH THAT MAN RIGHT OUTA MY HAIR,
AND SEND HIM ON HIS WAY.

*(**NELLIE** covers her eyes.)*

DON'T TRY TO PATCH IT UP,
TEAR IT UP, TEAR IT UP,
WASH HIM OUT, DRY HIM OUT,
PUSH HIM OUT, FLY HIM OUT,
CANCEL HIM, AND LET HIM GO –
YEA, SISTER!

(He finishes, waving his arms wildly.)

NELLIE. *(Applauding.)* That's wonderful, Emile.

*(**EMILE** lifts the cape and, looking off, sees **NGANA** and **JEROME** as they enter in their nightgowns, followed by **HENRY**.)*

EMILE. Bon soir!

(**NELLIE** *turns, looks at the* **CHILDREN**, *and is immediately enchanted. She kneels before the two of them, holding them at arm's length.*)

NELLIE. You're the cutest things I ever saw in my whole life! What are your names? You probably can't understand a word I'm saying, but, oh, my goodness, you're cute.

EMILE. Nellie, I want you to meet Ngana and Jerome. Ngagna and Jerome, Nellie.

NGANA & JEROME. Nellie...

EMILE. *(To the* **CHILDREN**.*)* Maintenant au lit...vite!

HENRY. Venez, Petits!

NGANA. Bon soir, Nellie.

JEROME. Bon soir, Nellie.

(*They wave to* **NELLIE** *as* **HENRY** *leads them out.*)

NELLIE. Bon soir!

(*Turning to* **EMILE**.*)* Oh, aren't they adorable! Those big black eyes staring at you out of those sweet little faces! Are they Henry's?

EMILE. They're mine.

NELLIE. *(Carrying out what she thinks is a joke.)* Oh, of course, they look exactly like you, don't they? Where did you hide their mother?

EMILE. She's dead, Nellie.

NELLIE. She's...

(*She turns.*)

Emile, they *are* yours!

EMILE. Yes, Nellie. I'm their father.

NELLIE. And...their mother...was a...was...a...

EMILE. Polynesian.

(**NELLIE** *is stunned. She turns away, trying to collect herself.*)

[MUSIC NO. 32 "FINALE ACT I"]

And she was beautiful, Nellie, and charming, too.

NELLIE. But you and she...

EMILE. I want you to know I have no apologies. I came here as a young man. I lived as I could.

NELLIE. Of course.

EMILE. But I have not been selfish. No woman ever hated me or tried to hurt me.

NELLIE. No woman could ever want to hurt you, Emile.

(Suddenly, feeling she must get away as quickly as she can.)

Oh, what time is it? I promised to get that jeep back!

(She looks at her wristwatch.)

Oh, this is awful. Look at the time!

(She grabs her cape. **EMILE** *tries to stop her.)*

EMILE. Nellie, wait, please. I'll drive you home.

NELLIE. You will do no such thing. Anyway, I couldn't leave the jeep here. I've got to get it back by...

EMILE. Don't go now, Nellie. Don't go yet, please.

NELLIE. *(Rattling on very fast.)* Oh, this is terrible! I won't be able to face the girls at the hospital. You can't imagine the way they look at you when you come in late... I'll call you, Emile. I'll come by tomorrow.

(Suddenly remembering.) Oh, no! Oh, dear! There are those awful rehearsals for Thanksgiving Day – I'm teaching them a dance and they want to rehearse night and day – but after that...

(Shifting quickly.) Oh, thank you for tonight, Emile. I had a wonderful time. It was the nicest party and you're a perfect host. Good-bye. Please stay here, Emile. Don't come out to the jeep, please.

EMILE. *(Grabbing her arms, feeling her slipping away from him.)* Nellie, I love you. Do you hear me, Nellie? I love you!

NELLIE. And I love you, too. Honestly I do... Please let me go! Please let me go!

(She runs off as fast as she can. **EMILE** *watches for a second. The motor of the jeep starts and fades away quickly, as though the jeep were driven away very, very fast. The music of "Some Enchanted Evening" swells as* **EMILE** *looks down and picks up a demitasse coffee cup that has been left on the fountain.)*

EMILE. *(With great conviction, as he looks down at the cup.)*
ONCE YOU HAVE FOUND HER,
NEVER LET HER GO.
ONCE YOU HAVE FOUND HER,
NEVER LET HER GO!

(The music swells as…)

(The curtain falls.)

ACT II

[MUSIC NO. 33 "ENTR'ACTE"]

Scene One
A Performance of "The Thanksgiving Follies"

(The "stage" during a performance of "The Thanksgiving Follies.")

[MUSIC NO. 34 "OPENING ACT II"]

(A dance is in progress. They meticulously perform the steps and evolutions of a dance routine no more distinguished or original than any that might be produced by a Navy nurse who had been the moving spirit in the amateur theatre of Little Rock. Not one of the dancers makes a single mistake. Nobody smiles. Tense concentration is evident in this laboriously perfect performance. During the course of the dance, there are solo "step-outs," after which the soloist soberly steps back into place. The most complicated unison step is saved for the exit, which they execute with vigorous precision. At one point **NELLIE** *shouts: "One, two, three, four, fix, six, seven, eight!")*

(On either side, in the downstage corners of the stage, **G.I.S** *are sitting as if there had not been enough seats and the audience overflowed up onto the stage. There are no chairs. They are seated and sprawled on the floor of the "stage".)*

*(The dance ends as **NELLIE** returns to the "stage," carrying a microphone and a sheaf of notes. She talks into the microphone.)*

NELLIE. It has been called to our attention that owing to some trouble with the mimeograph, the last part of the program is kind of blurry, so I will read off who did the last number.

(Reading.)

The hand-stand was by Marine Sergeant Johnson.

(Applause.)

The barrel roll was done by Lieutenant J.G. Bessie May Sue Ellie Yaeger.

(Applause.)

The solo featuring the hitch-kick and scissors – those are the names of the steps – was by Ensign Cora MacRae.

(Applause.)

The Pin Wheel – you know...

(She demonstrates by waving her leg in imitation of Stewpot.)

...was by Stewpot... I mean George Watts, Carpenter's Mate, Third Class.

*(Applause. **STEWPOT**'s head protrudes from the wings.)*

STEWPOT. Second Class!

(Applause and cat-calls.)

NELLIE. The multiple revolutions and,

(She becomes self-consciously modest.)

...incidentally, the dance steps were by Ensign Nellie Forbush.

(She bows. Applause.)

Now the next is a most unusual treat. An exhibition of weightlifting by Marine Staff Sergeant Thomas Hassinger.

(**HASSINGER** *enters from right. He flexes his muscles. Applause and shouts from the* **G.I. AUDIENCE** *on the corners of the stage.*)

SAILOR. Atta boy, Muscles!

(*The "stage" lights start fading.*)

NELLIE. ...And Sergeant Johnson,

(**JOHNSON** *enters.*)

...Marine Corporal...

(*The lights are out.*)

VOICE IN THE DARK. Hey, lights...

(*The* **G.I. AUDIENCE** *shines flashlights out front around the audience to cover the scene change.*)

...the lights are out... Billis!

NELLIE. Billis...what the heck happened to the lights?

OTHER VOICES. It's the generator run out of gas... Switch over to the other one... Mike...turn on the truck lights.

NELLIE. (*Offstage, over microphone.*) Keep your seats, everybody! There's nothing wrong except that the lights went out.

SAILOR. (*Flashing light in* **STEWPOT**'s *face.*) Look where you're going.

STEWPOT. (*Shining his light in the* **SAILOR**'s *face.*) How the hell can I look when I can't see?

Scene Two
Backstage at "The Thanksgiving Follies"

(The lights come up. The set has been changed in the darkness, and we are now in back of the "stage.")

MARINE. We'll have the other generator on in a minute.

BILLIS. They got the truck light on. That's something.

(Applause offstage right.)

STEWPOT. *(Looking off toward the "stage.")* The weightlifting act got started.

BILLIS. Good...

*(He notices two **SEABEES** carrying two large jerry cans each.)*

What I can't understand is how some guys ain't got the artistic imagination to put gas in a generator so a show can be a success – especially when they're on the committee.

SEABEE. You're on the committee, too. Why didn't you tell us it wasn't gassed up?

BILLIS. I'm acting in the show and I'm stage manager and producer. I can't figure out everything, can I?

SEABEE. Sure you can. Just put your two heads together.

*(The **SEABEES** exit, carrying the jerry cans.)*

BILLIS. *(Calling off.)* Look, jerk! I got a production on my hands.

*(Turning to **STEWPOT**.)* How's the weightlifting act going?

STEWPOT. I can't tell. Nobody's clapping.

BILLIS. If nobody's clapping, it ain't going good. You ought to be able to figure that out. Put your two heads together.

STEWPOT. You was the one with the two heads.

*(**EMILE** enters. He carries a bunch of flowers in his hand.)*

EMILE. Pardon, can you tell me where I can find Miss Forbush?

BILLIS. *(Shrewdly sensing trouble and determined to protect Nellie.)* She's onstage now. She's the emcee. She can't talk to nobody right now. Do you want me to take the flowers in to her?

EMILE. No. I would prefer to give them to her myself.

BILLIS. Are you Mister de Becque?

EMILE. Yes.

BILLIS. Look, Mister de Becque. Do me a favor, will you? Don't try and see her tonight.

EMILE. Why?

BILLIS. We got her in a great mood tonight and I don't want anything to upset her again.

EMILE. She has been upset?

BILLIS. Upset! She's asked for a transfer to another island. And day before yesterday, she busted out crying in the middle of rehearsal. Said she couldn't go on with the show. And she wouldn't have either unless Captain Brackett talked to her and told her how important it was to the base. So do us all a favor – don't try to see her now.

EMILE. She has asked for a transfer?

BILLIS. Don't tell her I told you. Nobody's supposed to know.

EMILE. I must see her. Tonight!

BILLIS. Then stay out of sight till after the show. I'll take the flowers to her.

>   *(**EMILE** gives him the flowers. **BILLIS** and **STEWPOT** exit. **CABLE** enters, his uniform sweat-stained and beads of sweat on his brow. He has been looking for **BILLIS**. He doesn't see **EMILE** at first.)*

CABLE. Hey, Billis – Billis!

EMILE. *(Peering through the semi-darkness.)* Lieutenant Cable?

[MUSIC NO. 35 "ENTRANCE OF LIAT"]

CABLE. *(Putting his fingers to his lips in a mocking gesture.)* Ssh! Lieutenant Cable is supposed to be in his little bed over at the hospital.

EMILE. You have not been well?

CABLE. I'm okay now. Fever gone. They can't hold me in that damned place any longer. I'm looking for a guy named Billis, a great guy for getting boats. *(His voice rising, tense and shrill.)* And I need a boat right now. I've got to get to my island.

EMILE. *(Worried by CABLE's strangeness.)* What?

CABLE. That damned island with the two volcanoes on it. You ever been over there?

EMILE. Why, yes, I...

CABLE. I went over there every day till this damned malaria stopped me. Have you sailed over early in the morning? With warm rain playing across your face?

> *(LIAT enters. CABLE sees her, but doesn't believe his eyes.)*

Beginning to see her again like last night.

LIAT. *(Calling offstage.)* Ma mere! C'est lui!

> *(Music stops. LIAT turns and, like a young doe, glides to the amazed CABLE and embraces him before the equally amazed EMILE. BLOODY MARY waddles on.)*

CABLE. *(Holding LIAT tight.)* I thought I was dreaming.

LIAT. *(Laughing.)* No.

> *(She holds him tighter.)*

CABLE. *(Holds her away from him and looks at her.)* What are you doing over here?

BLOODY MARY. *(Grimly.)* She come in big white boat – bigger than your boat. Belong Jacques Barrere. He want to marry Liat.

(To EMILE.) You know him.

(**EMILE** *nods.* **BLOODY MARY** *turns back to* **CABLE**.)

Is white man, too. And very rich!

CABLE. *(To* **LIAT**.*)* Is that the old planter you told me about? The one who drinks?

> *(His eye catches* **EMILE***'s.* **EMILE** *nods.* **CABLE** *cries out as if hurt.)*

Oh, my God!

> *(He turns angrily to* **BLOODY MARY**.*)*

You can't let her marry a man like that.

BLOODY MARY. Hokay! Then you marry her.

EMILE. *(Angrily, to* **BLOODY MARY**.*)* Tais-toi! Il est malade! ...Tu comprends?

> *(***BLOODY MARY*** is temporarily silenced.* **EMILE** *turns to* **CABLE**, *and his voice becomes gentle and sympathetic.)*

Lieutenant, I am worried about you. You are ill. Will you allow me to see you back to the hospital?

CABLE. You're worried about me! That's funny. The fellow who says he lives on an island all by himself and doesn't worry about anybody – Japanese, Americans, Germans – anybody. Why pick out me to worry about?

EMILE. *(Stiffly.)* Forgive me. I'm sorry, Lieutenant.

> *(He bows and leaves.* **CABLE** *moves as if to follow him and apologize.* **LIAT** *crosses in front of him and looks in his face. He melts and takes her in his arms.* **BLOODY MARY** *goes to* **CABLE** *to make one last plea for her daughter's dream.)*

BLOODY MARY. Lootellan, you like Liat... Marry Liat! You have good life here. Look, Lootellan, I am rich. I save six hundred dolla' before war. Since war I make two thousand dolla' – war go on I make maybe more. Sell grass skirts, boars' teeth, real human heads. Give all de money to you an' Liat. You no have to work. I work for you.

[MUSIC NO. 36 "HAPPY TALK"]

BLOODY MARY. All day long, you and Liat be together! Walk through woods, swim in sea, sing, dance, talk happy. No think about Philadelia. Is no good. Talk about beautiful things and make love all day long. You like? You buy?

HAPPY TALK,
KEEP TALKIN' HAPPY TALK!
TALK ABOUT TINGS YOU'D LIKE TO DO.
YOU GOT TO HAVE A DREAM;
IF YOU DON' HAVE A DREAM,
HOW YOU GONNA HAVE A DREAM COME TRUE?

TALK ABOUT A MOON
FLOATIN' IN DE SKY,
LOOKIN' LIKE A LILY ON A LAKE;
TALK ABOUT A BIRD
LEARNIN' HOW TO FLY,
MAKIN' ALL DE MUSIC HE CAN MAKE.

HAPPY TALK,
KEEP TALKIN' HAPPY TALK!
TALK ABOUT TINGS YOU'D LIKE TO DO.
YOU GOT TO HAVE A DREAM;
IF YOU DON' HAVE A DREAM
HOW YOU GONNA HAVE A DREAM COME TRUE?

TALK ABOUT A STAR
LOOKIN' LIKE A TOY,
PEEKIN' T'ROUGH DE BRANCHES OF A TREE.
TALK ABOUT A GIRL,
TALK ABOUT A BOY,
COUNTIN' ALL DE RIPPLES ON DE SEA.

HAPPY TALK,
KEEP TALKIN' HAPPY TALK!
TALK ABOUT TINGS YOU'D LIKE TO DO.
YOU GOT TO HAVE A DREAM;
IF YOU DON' HAVE A DREAM
HOW YOU GONNA HAVE A DREAM COME TRUE?

(LIAT now performs a gentle, childlike dance. At the end of it, she returns to CABLE's side and BLOODY MARY resumes her song.)

TALK ABOUT A BOY
SAYIN' TO DE GIRL:
"GOLLY, BABY, I'M A LUCKY CUSS!"
TALK ABOUT A GIRL
SAYIN' TO DE BOY:
"YOU AN' ME IS LUCKY TO BE US!"

(LIAT and CABLE kiss.)

HAPPY TALK,
KEEP TALKIN' HAPPY TALK!
TALK ABOUT TINGS YOU'D LIKE TO DO.
YOU GOT TO HAVE A DREAM;
IF YOU DON' HAVE A DREAM
HOW YOU GONNA HAVE A DREAM COME TRUE?

IF YOU DON' TALK HAPPY
AN' YOU NEVER HAVE A DREAM
DEN YOU'LL NEVER HAVE A DREAM COME TRUE.

(Speaking eagerly.) Is good idea – you like?

(She laughs heartily.)

[MUSIC NO. 37 "INCIDENTAL"]

(BLOODY MARY looks into CABLE's eyes, anxious to see his answer, to see if she has been successful in making the pairing. CABLE is deeply disturbed. He takes a gold watch from his pocket and puts it in LIAT's hand.)

CABLE. Liat, I want you to have this. It's a man's watch but it's a good one – belonged to my grandfather. It's kind of a lucky piece, too. My dad carried it all through the last war. Beautiful, isn't it?

(LIAT has taken the watch, her eyes gleaming with pride.)

BLOODY MARY. When I see you firs' time, I know you good man for Liat. And she good girl for you. You have special good babies.

> (*There is a loud orchestral sting of the first notes of "Happy Talk." A pause.*)

CABLE. (*Forcing the words out.*) Mary, I can't...marry...Liat.

BLOODY MARY. (*Letting out her rage and disappointment in a shout as she grabs* **LIAT**'s *arm.*) Was your las' chance! Now she marry Jacques Barrere. Come Liat!

> (**LIAT** *runs to* **CABLE**. **BLOODY MARY** *pulls her away.*)

Give me watch.

> (**LIAT** *clasps it tight in her hands.* **BLOODY MARY** *wrests it from her and yells at* **CABLE**.)

Stingy bastard!!

> (*She throws it on the ground and it smashes.* **CABLE** *looks on, dazed.* **LIAT** *tries to run to* **CABLE**, *but* **BLOODY MARY** *grabs her before she can. They exit.* **CABLE** *kneels down, gathers up the pieces of the watch, and puts them in his pocket. Meanwhile, several of the* **MEN**, *including the* **PROFESSOR** *and* **STEWPOT**, *come on, dressed for the finale of "The Thanksgiving Follies." They are looking back over their shoulders at* **LIAT** *and* **BLOODY MARY**, *whom they must have just passed.*)

PROFESSOR. Hey! Did you get a load of that little Tonkinese girl?

> (*They continue up to the "stage" door as they speak.*)

STEWPOT. Yeah.

> (*Applause offstage.* **NELLIE**'s *voice is heard through the loudspeaker.*)

NELLIE. *(Offstage.)* Now, boys, before we come to the last act of our show, it is my great pleasure to bring you our skipper, Captain Brackett.

> *(Applause.* **CABLE** *has been looking off at* **LIAT** *as she passes out of his life.)*

CABLE.
> YOUNGER THAN SPRINGTIME, WERE YOU,
> SOFTER THAN STARLIGHT, WERE YOU.
> ANGEL AND LOVER, HEAVEN AND EARTH
> WERE YOU TO ME...

> *(The lights fade to black.* **BRACKETT**'s *voice is heard over the loudspeaker:)*

Scene Three
The Performance Resumes, as in Scene One

> *(After his line the lights come up, revealing the G.I. "stage," as before, with **BRACKETT** speaking into the standing microphone at center stage. The **MEN** onstage, so lively and enthusiastic when last seen, are now in a state of almost total apathy.)*

BRACKETT. Up to now, our side has been having the hell beat out of it in two hemispheres and we're not going to get to go home until the situation is reversed.

> *(The lights come up.)*

It may take a long time before we can get any big operation under way, so it's things like this, like this show tonight, that keep us going. Now I understand that I am not generally considered a sentimental type.

VOICES. Oh, boy! You can say that again!

BRACKETT. Once or twice I understand I have been referred to as "Old Iron Belly."

VOICES. Once or twice! Just about a million times.

BRACKETT. I resent that very much because I had already chosen that as my private name for our Executive Officer, Commander Harbison.

> *(Big laugh. Applause. He calls into wings.)*

Take a bow, Commander.

> *(Two of the **GIRLS** pull **HARBISON** out.)*

SAILOR. I wish I was a commander!

> *(**HARBISON**, flanked by the two **GIRLS**, stands beside **BRACKETT** as he continues.)*

BRACKETT. I want you to know that both "Old Iron Bellies" sat here tonight and had a hell of a good time. And we want to thank that hardworking committee of Nurses and Seabees who made the costumes out of rope and mosquito nets, comic books and newspapers...

*(He fingers the paper skirt of one of the **GIRLS**.)*

SAILOR. Ah, ah – Captain!

*(**BRACKETT** frowns but pulls himself together.)*

BRACKETT. ...And thought up these jokes and these grand songs. And I just want to say on this Thanksgiving Day, to all of them from all of us, thank you.

*(The comically feeble applause from the **G.I. AUDIENCE** makes it obvious they'd like to get on with the show.)*

And now I'm going to ask Commander Harbison to announce the next act which is the finale of our Thanksgiving entertainment.

*(He hands **HARBISON** a small card. **HARBISON** reads from it.)*

HARBISON. The next and last will be a song sung by Bosun Butch Forbush...

(He looks kind of puzzled.)

...and that Siren of the Coral Sea – gorgeous, voluptuous and petite Mademoiselle Lutheria...

(A surprised voice, as he reads the name of his pet abomination.)

...Billis!

[MUSIC NO. 38 "HONEY BUN"]

BRACKETT. *(Laughing.)* Come on, Bill.

*(He leads off **HARBISON**, who takes the microphone with him. **NELLIE** enters, dressed in a borrowed white sailor suit at least three sizes too big for her.)*

NELLIE.
MY DOLL IS AS DAINTY AS A SPARROW,
HER FIGURE IS SOMETHING TO APPLAUD.
WHERE SHE'S NARROW, SHE'S NARROW AS AN ARROW
AND SHE'S BROAD

WHERE A BROAD
SHOULD BE BROAD!

*(Whistles and cheers from the **G.I. AUDIENCE**.)*

A HUNDRED AND ONE
POUNDS OF FUN –
THAT'S MY LITTLE HONEY BUN!
GET A LOAD OF HONEY BUN TONIGHT!

I'M SPEAKIN' OF MY
SWEETIE PIE,
ONLY SIXTY INCHES HIGH –
EVERY INCH IS PACKED WITH DYNAMITE!

HER HAIR IS BLONDE AND CURLY,
HER CURLS ARE HURLY-BURLY.
HER LIPS ARE PIPS!
I CALL HER HIPS:
"TWIRLY" AND "WHIRLY."

SHE'S MY BABY,
I'M HER PAP!
I'M HER BOOBY,
SHE'S MY TRAP!
I AM CAUGHT AND DON'T WANTA RUN
'CAUSE I'M HAVIN' SO MUCH FUN WITH HONEY BUN!

(She is having considerable difficulty with her sagging trousers.)

A HUNDRED AND ONE
POUNDS OF FUN –
THAT'S MY LITTLE HONEY BUN!
GET A LOAD OF HONEY BUN TONIGHT!
I'M SPEAKIN' OF MY SWEETIE PIE,

*(**BILLIS** enters, dressed as a South Sea siren in a straw-colored wig, long lashes fantastically painted on his eyelids, lips painted in bright carmine, two coconut shells on his chest to simulate femininity, a grass skirt, and a battleship tattooed on his bare midriff. The **G.I. AUDIENCE** rags **BILLIS** mercilessly with*

ad-libs: "Who does your hair? The laundry!"
"Get a load of those coconuts!" etc.)

ONLY SIXTY INCHES HIGH –
EVERY INCH IS PACKED WITH DYNAMITE!

HER HAIR IS BLONDE AND CURLY,
HER CURLS ARE HURLY-BURLY.
HER LIPS ARE PIPS!
I CALL HER HIPS:
"TWIRLY" AND "WHIRLY."

(She and **BILLIS** *dance.)*

I AM CAUGHT AND DON'T WANTA RUN
'CAUSE I'M HAVIN' SO MUCH FUN WITH HONEY BUN.
I AM CAUGHT AND DON'T WANTA RUN
'CAUSE I'M HAVIN' SO MUCH FUN WITH HONEY BUN.
(BELIEVE ME, SONNY!)
SHE'S A COOKIE WHO CAN COOK YOU TILL YOU'RE DONE.
(AIN'T BEIN' FUNNY!)
SONNY, PUT YOUR MONEY
ON MY HONEY BUN!

(Music stops. They exit. Then **NELLIE** *returns for a bow. Her trousers are still falling down, so she steps through her sailor tie to help keep the pants up. Music continues.* **BILLIS** *enters with Emile's flowers and presents them to her. Thinking they are from* **BILLIS**, *she kisses him. He exits in a delirious daze. She exits as the* **NURSES** *enter, dressed in homemade costumes representing island natives. The materials are fish net, parachute cloth, large tropical leaves, and flowers – anything they could find and sew together. At the end of their line is* **BILLIS**, *still in his costume.)*

NURSES.

A HUNDRED AND ONE
POUNDS OF FUN –
THAT'S MY LITTLE HONEY BUN!
GET A LOAD OF HONEY BUN TONIGHT!

I'M SPEAKIN' OF MY
SWEETIE PIE,

BILLIS.

ONLY SIXTY INCHES HIGH –

> *(A **G.I.** gooses **BILLIS**. He turns to swing on the **G.I.**, but he can't get out of line and spoil the number: "On with the show!" He is grim and stoic – even when another **MAN** lifts one of his coconuts and steals a package of cigarettes therefrom. The **NURSES** and **BILLIS** continue singing through these impromptu shenanigans.)*

NURSES & BILLIS.

EVERY INCH IS PACKED WITH DYNAMITE!
HER HAIR IS BLONDE AND CURLY,
HER CURLS ARE HURLY-BURLY.
HER LIPS ARE PIPS!
I CALL HER HIPS:
"TWIRLY" AND "WHIRLY."

> *(Undulating drum beat begins Billis' dance. He rolls his stomach so the ship tattooed on his belly seems to be having a stormy go of it. When "Anchors Away" is heard, the belly keeps going while **BILLIS** brings his hand up in proper patriotic salute.)*

SHE'S MY BABY,
I'M HER PAP!
I'M HER BOOBY,
SHE'S MY TRAP!

BILLIS.

I AM CAUGHT AND DON'T WANTA RUN

NURSES & BILLIS.

'CAUSE I'M HAVIN' SO MUCH FUN WITH HONEY BUN!

> *(**ALL** lining up for the finale.)*

AND THAT'S THE FINISH,
AND IT'S TIME TO GO FOR NOW THE SHOW IS DONE.

(Balance of the "Follies" cast comes on.)

WE HOPE YOU LIKED US,
AND WE HOPE THAT WHEN YOU LEAVE YOUR SEAT AND RUN
DOWN TO THE MESS HALL
YOU'LL ENJOY YOUR DINNER EACH AND EVERY ONE.

NELLIE. *(Making a special entrance, now wearing a new costume.)*

SAVE ME SOME TURKEY!

ALL. *(Pointing to* **BILLIS.***)*

AND PUT SOME CHESTNUT DRESSING ON OUR HONEY BUN!

> *(The curtain is slow.* **NELLIE** *signals for it and jumps up to help pull it down as the lights fade to black.* **G.I.S** *wave their flashlights out at the audience, addressing them as if they were all* **G.I.S***: "See you down at the mess hall," etc. When the clamor dies down, the following two lines are distinguishable.)*

SAILOR. How d'ya like the show?

MARINE. It stunk!

Scene Four
Backstage, as in Scene Two

(Again, the lights come up on the backstage area. **CABLE** *is seated on a bench below the dressing tent. The* **GIRLS** *come off the "stage" and file into their dressing tent.* **BILLIS** *follows them in. After a few moments, he comes hurling out, minus his wig. A few seconds later, the wig comes flying out, thrown by one of the* **GIRLS** *in the dressing tent.)*

BILLIS. Oh, beg your pardon.

(At this moment, he turns and faces **NELLIE**, *who has just come down the steps from the stage with* **DINAH**.*)*

NELLIE. *(Seeing* **BILLIS**.*)* Oh, Luther, you really are a honey bun! These beautiful flowers! I needed someone to think of me tonight. I appreciate it, Luther – you don't know how much.

BILLIS. *(Very emotional.)* Miss Forbush, I would like you to know I consider you the most wonderful woman in the entire world – even including the fact that you're an officer and all. And I just can't go on being such a heel as to let you think I thought of giving you those flowers.

NELLIE. But you did give them to me and I...

BILLIS. *(Shoving card at* **NELLIE**.*)* Here's the card that came with them.

*(***NELLIE** *reads the card then turns away, deeply affected.)*

Are you all right, Miss Forbush?

*(***NELLIE** *nods her head.)*

I'll be waiting around the area here in case you need me. Just...just sing out.

(He exits. **NELLIE** *is on the verge of tears.)*

CABLE. *(Sympathetically, but taking a light tone.)* What's the matter, Nellie the nurse? Having diplomatic difficulties with France?

> *(NELLIE turns, startled. Then crosses to CABLE, becoming the professional nurse.)*

NELLIE. Joe Cable! Who let you out of the hospital?

CABLE. Me. I'm okay.

NELLIE. *(She feels CABLE's forehead and pulse.)* Joe! You're trying to get over to Bali Ha'i. That little girl you told me about!

CABLE. *(Nodding thoughtfully.)* Liat. I've just seen her for the last time, I guess. I love her and yet I just heard myself saying I can't marry her. What's the matter with me, Nellie? What kind of guy am I, anyway?

NELLIE. You're all right. You're just far away from home. We're both so far from home.

> *(She looks at the card. CABLE takes her hand. EMILE enters. He is earnest and importunate.)*

EMILE. Nellie! I must see you.

NELLIE. Emile! I...

EMILE. Will you excuse us, Lieutenant Cable?

> *(CABLE starts to rise.)*

NELLIE. *(With a hand on CABLE's shoulder.)* No, wait a minute, Joe. Stay. Please!

(To EMILE.) I've been meaning to call you but...

EMILE. You have asked for a transfer, why? What does it mean?

NELLIE. I'll explain it to you tomorrow, Emile. I'm...

EMILE. No. Now. What does it mean, Nellie?

NELLIE. It means that I can't marry you. Do you understand? I can't marry you.

EMILE. Nellie... Because of my children?

NELLIE. Not because of your children. They're sweet.

EMILE. It is their Polynesian mother then – their mother and I.

NELLIE. ...Yes. I can't help it. It isn't as if I could give you a good reason. There is no reason. This is emotional. This is something that is born in me.

EMILE. *(Shouting the words in bitter protest.)* It is not. I do not believe this is born in you.

NELLIE. Then why do I feel the way I do? All I know is that I can't help it. I can't help it! Explain how we feel, Joe.

> (**CABLE** *gives her no help. She runs up to the door of the dressing tent.*)

EMILE. Nellie!

NELLIE. *(Calling in.)* Dinah, are you ready?

DINAH. Yes, Nellie.

NELLIE. I'll go with you.

> (**DINAH** *comes out and they exit quickly.* **EMILE** *turns angrily to* **CABLE**.)

EMILE. What makes her talk like that? Why do you have this feeling, you and she? I do not believe it is born in you. I do not believe it.

CABLE. It's not born in you!

[MUSIC NO. 39 "YOU'VE GOT TO BE CAREFULLY TAUGHT"]

It happens after you're born...

> *(He sings as if figuring this whole question out for the first time.)*

YOU'VE GOT TO BE TAUGHT TO HATE AND FEAR,
YOU'VE GOT TO BE TAUGHT FROM YEAR TO YEAR,
IT'S GOT TO BE DRUMMED IN YOUR DEAR LITTLE EAR –
YOU'VE GOT TO BE CAREFULLY TAUGHT!

YOU'VE GOT TO BE TAUGHT TO BE AFRAID
OF PEOPLE WHOSE EYES ARE ODDLY MADE,
AND PEOPLE WHOSE SKIN IS A DIFFERENT SHADE –
YOU'VE GOT TO BE CAREFULLY TAUGHT.

YOU'VE GOT TO BE TAUGHT BEFORE IT'S TOO LATE,
BEFORE YOU ARE SIX OR SEVEN OR EIGHT,
TO HATE ALL THE PEOPLE YOUR RELATIVES HATE –
YOU'VE GOT TO BE CAREFULLY TAUGHT!
YOU'VE GOT TO BE CAREFULLY TAUGHT!

[MUSIC NO. 39A "YOU'VE GOT TO BE CAREFULLY TAUGHT (CONTINUED)"]

EMILE. This is just the kind of ugliness I was running away from. It has followed me all this way – all these years – now it has found me.

I WAS CHEATED BEFORE
AND I'M CHEATED AGAIN
BY A MEAN LITTLE WORLD
OF MEAN LITTLE MEN.

AND THE ONE CHANCE FOR ME
IS THE LIFE I KNOW BEST,
TO BE HERE ON AN ISLAND
AND TO HELL WITH THE REST.
I WILL CLING TO THIS ISLAND
LIKE A TREE OR A STONE,
I WILL CLING TO THIS ISLAND
AND BE FREE – AND ALONE.

[MUSIC NO. 40 "INCIDENTAL BRIDGE"]

CABLE. Yes, sir, if I get out of this thing alive, I'm not going back there. I'm coming here. All I care about is right here.

EMILE. *(Thoughtfully.)* When all you care about is here, this is a good place to be. When all you care about is taken away from you, there is no place...

> *(Walking away from* **CABLE**, *now talking to himself.)*

I came so close to it...so close.

[MUSIC NO. 41 "THIS NEARLY WAS MINE"]

ONE DREAM IN MY HEART,
ONE LOVE TO BE LIVING FOR,

ONE LOVE TO BE LIVING FOR –
THIS NEARLY WAS MINE.

ONE GIRL FOR MY DREAM,
ONE PARTNER IN PARADISE,
THIS PROMISE OF PARADISE –
THIS NEARLY WAS MINE.

CLOSE TO MY HEART SHE CAME,
ONLY TO FLY AWAY,
ONLY TO FLY AS DAY
FLIES FROM MOONLIGHT!

NOW, NOW I'M ALONE,
STILL DREAMING OF PARADISE,
STILL SAYING THAT PARADISE
ONCE NEARLY WAS MINE.

SO CLEAR AND DEEP ARE MY FANCIES
OF THINGS I WISH WERE TRUE,
I'LL KEEP REMEMBERING EVENINGS
I WISH I'D SPENT WITH YOU.
I'LL KEEP REMEMBERING KISSES
FROM LIPS I'LL NEVER OWN
AND ALL THE LOVELY ADVENTURES
THAT WE HAVE NEVER KNOWN.

ONE DREAM IN MY HEART,
ONE LOVE TO BE LIVING FOR,
ONE LOVE TO BE LIVING FOR –
THIS NEARLY WAS MINE.

ONE GIRL FOR MY DREAM,
ONE PARTNER IN PARADISE,
THIS PROMISE OF PARADISE –
THIS NEARLY WAS MINE.

CLOSE TO MY HEART SHE CAME,
ONLY TO FLY AWAY,
ONLY TO FLY AS DAY
FLIES FROM MOONLIGHT!
NOW...NOW I'M ALONE,
STILL DREAMING OF PARADISE,

STILL SAYING THAT PARADISE
ONCE NEARLY WAS MINE.

[MUSIC NO. 42 "AFTER EMILE'S SOLO"]

CABLE. De Becque, would you reconsider going up there with me to Marie Louise Island? I mean, now that you haven't got so much to lose? We could do a good job, I think – you and I.

> (**EMILE** *doesn't answer.*)

You know, back home when I used to get in a jam, I used to go hunting. That's what I think I'll do now. Good hunting up there around Marie Louise. Japanese carriers…cargo boats…troopships – big game.

> (*He looks at* **EMILE**, *considering how much headway he has made.*)

When I go up, what side of the island should I land on?

EMILE. The south side.

CABLE. Why?

EMILE. There's a cove there…and rocks. I have sailed in behind these rocks many times.

CABLE. Could a submarine get in between those rocks without being observed?

EMILE. Yes. If you know the channel.

CABLE. And after I land, what will I do?

EMILE. You will get in touch with my friends, Basile and Inato – two Black men – wonderful hunters. They will hide us in the hills.

> (*The music stops.*)

CABLE. (*His eyes lighting up.*) Us? Are you going with me?

EMILE. (*A new strength in his voice.*) Of course. You are too young to be out alone. Let's go and find Captain Brackett.

> (*He starts to exit.*)

CABLE. (*Following* **EMILE**.) Wait till that old bastard Brackett hears this. He'll jump out of his skin!

EMILE. I would like to see this kind of a jump. Come on!

[MUSIC NO. 43 "THE TAKEOFF"]

(They go off quickly together. **BILLIS** *rushes on and looks after them. Obviously he's been listening. He thinks it over for a moment. Then, with sudden decision, he takes one last puff on a cigarette, stomps it out, and follows after them. Blackout.)*

Scene Five
Another Part of the Island

(Almost immediately following, the sound of an airplane motor is heard, revving up, ready for takeoff. The lights come up between the tapa-cloth and the dark-green drop. Several Naval Aircraft **MECHANICS** *with signal lamps [long-beam flashlights] are standing with their backs to the audience. They look off, watching tensely. As the plane is heard taking off, they follow the plane with their flashlights and shout: "There it is," "There she goes," "Come on," etc. The music reaches a climax, and the lights fade out on the* **MECHANICS** *as they exit. Radio static is heard in the darkness as the lights come up center stage.)*

Scene Six
The Radio Shack

(The radio shack. The back wall is covered with communications equipment of all sorts: boards, lights, switches, a speaker. Right is a small table with a receiving set, various telephones, and sending equipment. **MCCAFFREY**, *the radio operator, is sitting at the table with earphones. He works the dials.* **BRACKETT** *is seated on an upturned wastebasket. On the floor are several empty Coca-Cola bottles and several full ones.* **BRACKETT** *is eating a sandwich and alternately guzzling from a bottle of Coca-Cola. There are a couple of empty Coca-Cola bottles and beer cans on McCaffrey's table.* **BRACKETT** *is listening avidly for any possible sound that might come from the loudspeaker. After a moment, there is a crackle.)*

BRACKETT. *(Excitedly.)* What's that? What's that?

*(***MCCAFFREY*** cannot hear him because he wears earphones.* **BRACKETT** *suddenly becomes conscious of this. He pokes* **MCCAFFREY** *in the back, who, controlling himself, turns and looks at* **BRACKETT***, as a nurse would look at an anxious, complaining patient. He removes the earphones.)*

What was that?

MCCAFFREY. *(Quietly.)* That was...nothing, sir.

(He readjusts his earphones and turns to his dials again. **BRACKETT***, unsatisfied by this, pokes* **MCCAFFREY** *again, who winces, then patiently takes the earphones from his ears.)*

BRACKETT. Sounded to me like someone trying to send a message – sounded like code.

MCCAFFREY. *(As if explaining to a child.)* That was no code, sir. That sound you just heard was the contraction of the tin roof. It's the metal, cooling off at night.

BRACKETT. Oh.

MCCAFFREY. Sir, if you'd like to go back to your office, I'll let you know as soon as...

BRACKETT. No, no, I'll stay right here. I don't want to add to your problems.

MCCAFFREY. *(Turning back to his dials.)* Yes, sir.

> *(BRACKETT impatiently looks at his watch and compares it with the watch on McCaffrey's desk.)*

BRACKETT. We ought to be getting a message now. We ought to be getting a message, that's all. They'd have time to land and establish some sort of an observation post by now, don't you think so?

> *(He realizes that MCCAFFREY cannot hear him.)*

Oh.

> *(HARBISON enters. He is very stern, more upset than we have ever seen him. He stands at the door.)*

HARBISON. Captain Brackett?

BRACKETT. Yeah, what is it? What is it? Don't interrupt me now, Bill. I'm very busy.

HARBISON. It's about this Seabee out here, sir, Billis! Commander Perkins over at Operations estimates that Billis' act this morning cost the Navy over six hundred thousand dollars!

BRACKETT. Six hundred... By God, I'm going to chew that guy's... Send him in here!

HARBISON. Yes, sir.

> *(He exits. BRACKETT goes over and taps MCCAFFREY on the shoulder. MCCAFFREY removes his earphones.)*

BRACKETT. Let me know the moment you get any word. No matter what I'm doing, you just break right in.

MCCAFFREY. Yes, sir.

> *(He goes back to work. **BRACKETT** paces another second, and then **BILLIS** enters, wary, on guard – he stands at attention; his face is flaming red, his nose is a white triangle covered in zinc oxide. He is naked to the waist. His arms are red except for two patches of zinc oxide on his shoulders; he wears an old pair of dungarees, the boar's-tooth bracelet, and a silver necklace. He is followed by **LIEUTENANT BUZZ ADAMS** and **HARBISON**, who closes the door.)*

HARBISON. *(Pushing **BILLIS** in.)* Get in there! Captain Brackett, this is Lieutenant Buzz Adams, who flew the mission.

BRACKETT. H'y'a Adams.

ADAMS. Captain.

> *(He salutes. **BRACKETT** beckons **BILLIS** to him. **BILLIS** walks over to him slowly, not knowing what may hit him. Nevertheless, he stands at attention.)*

BRACKETT. One man like you in an outfit is like a rotten apple in a barrel. Just what did you feel like – sitting down there all day long in that little rubber boat in the middle of Empress Augusta Bay with the whole damn Navy Air Force trying to rescue you? And how the hell can you fall out of a PBY anyway?

BILLIS. Well, sir, the enemy anti-aircraft busted a hole in the side of the plane and I fell through – the wind just sucked me out.

BRACKETT. *(Pacing.)* So I'm to understand that you deliberately hid in the baggage compartment of a plane that you knew was taking off on a very dangerous mission. You had sand enough to do that all right. And then the moment an anti-aircraft gun hit the plane... you fell out. The wind just sucked you out – you and your little parachute! I don't think you fell out, Billis, I think you jumped out. Which did you do?

BILLIS. Well, sir...er...it was sort of half and half...if you get the picture.

BRACKETT. This is one of the most humiliating things that ever happened to me. Adams, when did you discover he was on the plane?

ADAMS. *(Accompanies the following speech with descriptive gestures.)* Well, sir, we'd been out about an hour – it was still dark, I know. Well, we were flying across Marie Louisa. The enemy anti-aircraft spotted us and made that hit. That's when Luther...er...this fellow here – that's when he...left the ship. I just circled once – time enough to drop him a rubber boat. Some New Zealanders in P-40s spotted him though and kept circling around him while I flew across the island and landed alongside the sub, let Joe and the Frenchman off. By the time I got back to the other side of the island, our Navy planes were flying around in the air above this guy like a thick swarm of bees.

> *(He turns to grin at **HARBISON**, who gives him no sympathy. He clears his throat and turns back to **BRACKETT**.)*

They kept the enemy guns occupied while I slipped down and scooped him off the rubber boat. You'd have thought this guy was a ninety-million dollar cruiser they were out to protect. There must have been fifty-five or sixty planes.

BILLIS. Sixty-two.

BRACKETT. You're not far off, Adams. Harbison tells me this thing cost the Navy about six hundred thousand dollars.

BILLIS. *(His face lighting up.)* Six hundred thous...!

BRACKETT. What the hell are you so happy about?

BILLIS. I was just thinking about my uncle.

BILLIS. *(To* **ADAMS.***)* Remember my uncle I was telling you about? He used to tell my old man I'd never be worth a dime!

(Turns to **HARBISON.***)* Him and his lousy slot machines... Can you imagine a guy...

*(***HARBISON** *scowls.* **BILLIS** *shuts up quickly.)*

BRACKETT. Why the hell did you do this anyway, Billis? What would make a man do a thing like this?

BILLIS. *(Again at attention.)* Well, sir, a fellow has to keep moving. You know, you get kind of held down. If you're itching to take a trip to pick up a few souvenirs, you got to kind of horn in – if you get the picture.

BRACKETT. How did you know about it?

BILLIS. I didn't know about it, exactly. It's just when I heard Lieutenant Cable talking to that fellow de Becque, right away I know something's in the air. A project. That's what I like, Captain.

(He stands easy, looks at **BRACKETT.***)*

Projects. Don't you?

HARBISON. *(Fuming.)* Billis, you've broken every regulation in the book. And, by God, Captain Brackett and I are going to throw it at you.

ADAMS. Sir. May I barge in? My co-pilot watched this whole thing, you know, and he thinks that this fellow Billis down there in the rubber boat with all those planes over him caused a kind of...diversionary action. While all those enemy were busy shooting at the planes and at Billis, on the other side of the island, that sub was sliding into that little cove and depositing the Frenchman and Joe Cable in behind those rocks.

BRACKETT. What the hell do you want me to do? Give this guy a Bronze Star?

BILLIS. I don't want any Bronze Star, Captain. But I could use a little freedom. A little room to swing around in – if you know what I mean. If you get the picture.

*(He looks at **BRACKETT**, who is not amused. He snaps to attention.)*

BRACKETT. Get out of here.

*(**BILLIS** crosses to the door, stops, and turns to **BRACKETT**.)*

Get the hell out of here!

BILLIS. Yes, sir!

(He exits.)

BRACKETT. Well, "Iron Belly," what would you have done?

HARBISON. I'd have thrown him in the brig. And I will, too, if get the ghost of a chance.

*(Suddenly, **MCCAFFREY** becomes very excited and waves his arms at **BRACKETT**. We begin to hear squeaks and static from the loudspeaker, and through it we hear **EMILE**'s voice. Everyone on the stage turns. All eyes and ears are focused on the loudspeaker.)*

EMILE'S VOICE. ...And so we are here. This is our first chance to send news to you. We have made contact with former friends of mine. We have set up quarters in a mango tree – no room but a lovely view. First the weather: rain clouds over Bougainville, the Treasuries, Choiseul and New Georgia. We expect rain in this region from nine o'clock to two o'clock. Pardon? Oh – my friend Joe corrects me. Oh – nine hundred to fourteen hundred. And now, our military expert, Joe.

CABLE'S VOICE. All you Navy, Marine, and Army pilots write this down.

*(**ADAMS** whips out a notebook and writes as **CABLE** speaks.)*

Surface craft – nineteen troop barges headed down the bottleneck; speed about eleven knots. Ought to pass Banika at about twenty hundred tonight, escorted by heavy warships.

(**BRACKETT** *and* **HARBISON** *smile triumphantly.*)

CABLE'S VOICE. There ought to be some way to knock off a few of these.

> (*His voice continues under the following speeches.*)

As for aircraft, there is little indication of activity at the moment. But twenty-two bombers – Betties – went by at 0600 headed southwest. There was fighter escort, not heavy...they should reach...

ADAMS. Oh, boy!

> (*He goes to the door.*)

HARBISON. Where you going?

ADAMS. Don't want to miss that takeoff. We'll be going out in waves tonight – waves.

> (*He exits quickly.*)

[MUSIC NO. 44 "COMMUNICATION ESTABLISHED"]

> (**BRACKETT** *sits down on the wastebasket and opens another Coke.*)

BRACKETT. Sit down, Bill.

> (**HARBISON** *sits, listening intently.* **BRACKETT** *hands him a Coke.* **HARBISON** *takes it.*)

Here.

HARBISON. Thanks.

BRACKETT. You know what I like, Bill? Projects – don't you?

> (*Lights start to fade.*)

Scene Seven
Another Part of the Island

(Lights cross-fade to extreme stage right, where a group of **PILOTS** *is gathered around a radio set. On the opposite side of the stage, in darkness, stands another group of* **PILOTS** *around a contour map.)*

1ST PILOT. Listen carefully.

EMILE'S VOICE. *(Coming from the radio.)* Ceiling today unlimited. Thirty-three fighters – Zeros – have moved in from Bougainville. Their course is approximately twenty-three degrees. Undoubtedly, heavy bombers will follow.

1ST PILOT. Got that?

(Lights cross-fade to the group around the map, which is now illuminated.)

2ND PILOT. Well, gentlemen, here's the hot tip for today. Joe and the Frenchman have sighted twenty surface craft heading southeast from Vella Lavella. Christmas is just two weeks away. Let's give those two characters a present – a beautiful view of no ships coming back.

3RD PILOT. Okay with me. Let's go!

(The music builds as they exit and the lights fade.)

Scene Eight
The Radio Shack

(The radio shack. **BRACKETT** *is pacing.* **HARBISON** *is standing near the door, a pleading expression on his face.)*

HARBISON. Sir, you just have to tell her something some time. She hasn't seen him for two weeks. She might as well know it now.

BRACKETT. Okay. Send her in. Send her in. I always have to do the tough jobs.

> *(***HARBISON** *exits. A second later,* **NELLIE** *enters, carrying a clipboard, followed by* **HARBISON**. **NELLIE** *goes to* **BRACKETT** *and immediately plunges into the subject closest to her heart. Her speech is unplanned. She knows she has no right to ask her question, but she must have an answer.)*

NELLIE. Captain Brackett, I know this isn't regular... It's about Emile de Becque. I went to his house a week ago to... You know how people have arguments and then days later you think of a good answer... Well, I went to his house, and he wasn't there. I even asked the children – he has two little children – and they didn't seem to know where he'd gone. At least, I think that's what they said – they only speak French. And then tonight while I was on duty in the ward – we have a lot of fighter pilots over there, the boys who knocked out that convoy yesterday – you know how fighter pilots talk...about "Immelmanns" and "wingovers" and things. I never listen usually but they kept talking about a Frenchman – the Frenchman said this, and the Frenchman said that...and I was wondering if this Frenchman they were talking about could be...my Frenchman.

> *(Pause.)*

BRACKETT. Yes, Miss Forbush, it is. I couldn't tell you before but... As a matter of fact, if you wait here a few minutes, you can hear his voice.

NELLIE. His voice? Where is he?

BRACKETT. With Lieutenant Cable behind enemy lines.

NELLIE. Behind...!

> (**MCCAFFREY** *snaps his fingers. All heads turn toward the loudspeaker. They listen to* **EMILE'S VOICE** *on the radio.*)

EMILE'S VOICE. Hello. Hello, my friends and allies. My message today must be brief...and sad. Lieutenant Cable, my friend, Joe, died last night. He died from wounds he received three days ago. I will never know a finer man. I wish he could have told you the good news. The Japanese are pulling out and there is great confusion. Our guess is that they will try to evacuate troops from Cape Esperance tonight. You may not hear from us for several days. We must move again. Two planes are overhead. They are looking for us, we think. We believe that...

> (*His speech is interrupted. There is the sound of a plane engine.* **EMILE'S VOICE** *is heard shouting excitedly "off mike."*)

What? ...What?

(*"On mike."*) Good-bye!

> (*There is a moment's silence.* **MCCAFFREY** *works the dials.*)

BRACKETT. Is that all? Is that all? Can't you get them back?

[MUSIC NO. 45 "COMMUNICATION DISCONTINUED"]

MCCAFFREY. No, sir. They're cut off.

NELLIE. Poor Joe. Poor little Joe Cable.

> (*She grabs* **BRACKETT** *and holds tightly to his arms.*)

NELLIE. Captain Brackett... Do you think there's a chance I'll ever see Emile de Becque again? If you don't think so, will you tell me?

BRACKETT. There's a chance...of course there's a chance.

NELLIE. *(Turning to* **HARBISON.***)* I didn't know he was going.

BRACKETT. Of course not. How could he tell you he was going? Now don't blame Emile de Becque. He's okay... he's a wonderful guy!

> *(These last words are underscored.* **NELLIE** *tries to answer, swallows hard, and can make only an inarticulate sound of assent.)*

NELLIE. Uh-huh!

> *(She exits quickly.)*

BRACKETT. He has got a chance, hasn't he, Bill?

HARBISON. *(Hoarsely.)* Of course. There's always a chance!

BRACKETT. Come on! Let's get out of here!

> *(Both exit as the shack recedes upstage, and the Company Street traveler comes in.)*

Scene Nine
The Company Street

(A group of **OFFICERS** *and* **NURSES** *enter downstage and walk across the Company Street on their way to a dance.* **NELLIE** *walks on from the opposite side, looking straight ahead of her, a set expression on her face.)*

NURSE. Coming to the dance, Nellie?

*(***NELLIE** *just shakes her head and passes them.)*

OFFICER (QUALE). What's the matter with her?

(In the spirit of kidding **NELLIE**, *the* **NURSES** *sing over their shoulders.)*

NURSES.
SHE'S IN LOVE, SHE'S IN LOVE,
SHE'S IN LOVE, SHE'S IN LOVE,
SHE'S IN LOVE... *(ETC.)*

*(***DINAH** *breaks away from her* **DATE** *and starts to follow* **NELLIE**. *Her* **DATE** *pulls her reluctantly back. The lights start to dim as the music rises in intensity.)*

Scene Ten
The Beach

*(The beach. **NELLIE** walks on, the strain of "I'm in Love..." ringing in her ears and cutting deeply into her heart. She walks up and looks over the sea. Pause. Then she speaks softly.)*

NELLIE. Come back so I can tell you something. I know what counts now. You. All those other things – the woman you had before – her color...

(She laughs bitterly.)

What piffle! What a pinhead I was! Come back so I can tell you. Oh, my God, don't die until I can tell you! All that matters is you and I being together. That's all! Just together – the way we wanted it to be the first night we met! Remember? ...Remember?

(She sing softly.)

SOME ENCHANTED EVENING
WHEN YOU FIND YOUR TRUE LOVE,
WHEN YOU FEEL HIM CALL YOU
ACROSS A CROWDED ROOM –
THEN FLY TO HIS SIDE,
AND MAKE HIM YOUR OWN,
OR ALL THROUGH YOUR LIFE YOU MAY DREAM ALL A...

(Her voice cracks. She speaks.)

Don't die, Emile.

*(Music continues. **BLOODY MARY** enters and addresses **NELLIE** timidly.)*

BLOODY MARY. Miss Nurse!

*(**NELLIE**, shocked by the sudden sound of an intruding voice, turns with a start.)*

Please, please, Miss Nurse?

NELLIE. Who are you? What do you want?

BLOODY MARY. Where is Lootellan Cable?

NELLIE. Who are you?

BLOODY MARY. I am mother of Liat.

NELLIE. Who?

BLOODY MARY. Liat. She won't marry no one but Lootellan Cable.

>*(**LIAT** walks on slowly. **BLOODY MARY** moves her forward and shows her to **NELLIE**. **NELLIE** looks at this girl and realizes who she is.)*

NELLIE. Oh.

>*(She rushes to **LIAT** impulsively and embraces her.)*

Oh, my darling!

>*(As she clasps **LIAT** in her arms, a strain of "Happy Talk" is heard from the orchestra, and lights fade. The music segues into:)*

[MUSIC NO. 46 "OPERATION ALLIGATOR"]

Scene Eleven
The Beach

(The Company Street is harshly noisy, crowded with **MEMBERS** *of all forces ready to embark. There are sounds of truck convoys passing.)*

VOICE ON LOUDSPEAKER. All right, hear this. All those outfits that are waiting for loading, please keep in position. We'll get to you as soon as your ship is ready for you.

*(***BILLIS**, **STEWPOT**, *and the* **PROFESSOR** *enter.)*

STEWPOT. Hey, Billis, let's head back, huh? Our gang's about a mile back down the beach. Suppose they call our names?

PROFESSOR. Yeah! They may be ready for us to go aboard.

BILLIS. They won't be ready for hours yet – this is the Navy.

(He turns and regards the scene offstage.)

Eager Beavers! Look at that beach...swarmin' with 10,000 guys – all jerks!

(Picking out a likely "jerk.")

Hey, Marine.

MARINE. Yeah!

BILLIS. Are you booked on one of those LCTs?

MARINE. I guess so, why?

BILLIS. They'll shake the belly off you, you know.

(He takes out a small package.)

Five bucks and you can have it.

MARINE. What is it?

BILLIS. Seasick remedy. You'll be needing it.

MARINE. Aw, knock it off!

(Pulls out a handful of packages from his pocket.)

That stuff's issued. We all got it. Who are you tryin' to fool?

BILLIS. *(To* **STEWPOT.***)* These Marines are getting smarter every day.

SHORE PATROLMAN. *(Passing through.)* All right, all right. Stay with your own unit.

(To **NURSE** *in combat uniform.)* Ensign, you too. For heaven's sake, don't get spread out over here. We're trying to get this thing organized as quickly as possible, so for God's sake, stay with your outfit!

(To **BILLIS.***)* Say, Seabee – you belong down the beach.

BILLIS. *(Saluting* **PATROLMAN.***)* Excuse me, sir, could you tell me where we could find Captain Brackett?

SHORE PATROLMAN. *(Returning salute.)* He's up at the head of the Company Street. He'll be along any minute now.

BILLIS. *(Ending salute.)* Thank you, sir. That's all, sir.

> *(The* **SHORE PATROLMAN**, *having started off, stops in his tracks, stunned and rocked off his balance by being thus "dismissed" by* **BILLIS**. *Oh, well – too many important things to be done right now! He goes on his way, shouting.)*

SHORE PATROLMAN. All right! Stay in line! How many times have I told you...

> *(He is off. A* **NURSE** *comes by.)*

BILLIS. Hello, Miss MacGregor. You nurses going too?

NURSE MACGREGOR. Only a few of us. We're going to fly back some wounded.

BILLIS. Is Miss Forbush going with you?

NURSE MACGREGOR. I don't know. She may be staying here with the hospital.

> *(She starts to leave.)*

BILLIS. Oh, Miss MacGregor – you don't get airsick, do you? I was thinking maybe if you got three bucks handy, you might be able to use this little package I got here.

NURSE MACGREGOR. *(Looking down at it.)* Oh, that stuff's no good – we gave that up last month.

BILLIS. *(Turning to* **STEWPOT.***)* That's a female jerk!

(**BRACKETT** *and* **HARBISON** *enter.*)

I beg pardon, sir...could I speak to you a moment?

BRACKETT. *(Peering through the semi-darkness.)* Who's that?

BILLIS. Billis, sir...Luther Billis.

BRACKETT. Oh. What do you want, Billis? We're moving out pretty soon.

BILLIS. Yes, sir, I know. I'd like to do something for Miss Forbush, sir. Stewpot and the Professor and me was wondering if anything is being done about rescuing the Frenchman off that island. We hereby volunteer for such a project – a triple diversionary activity, like I done to get 'em on there. You could drop us in three rubber boats on three different sides of the island – confuse the hell out of the enemy. Get the picture?

BRACKETT. It's very fine of you, Billis...but you're too late for diversionary activity. That started this morning before the sun came up.

[MUSIC NO. 47 "INCIDENTAL"]

Operation Alligator got under way. Landings were made on fourteen Japanese-held islands.

BILLIS. I think that's very unfair, sir. The first thing they should have done was try to rescue that Frenchman.

HARBISON. The Admiral agrees with you, Billis. Marie Louise was the first island they hit.

BILLIS. Did they get him? Is he alive?

BRACKETT. We don't know. Lieutenant Buzz Adams flew up there to find out. He hasn't come back. But if the Frenchman's dead, it is unfair. It's too damned bad if a part of this huge operation couldn't have saved one of the two guys who made it all possible.

HARBISON. *(Gazing off.)* Look at the beach – far as you can see – men waiting to board ships. The whole picture of the South Pacific has changed. We're going the other way.

SHORE PATROLMAN. Captain Brackett, sir – the launch is ready to take your ship.

BILLIS. *(Amazed.)* You got a ship, sir?

BRACKETT. Yes, Harbison and I've got a ship. I'm no longer a lousy Island Commander. Come on, Bill.

BILLIS. Good-bye, Commander Harbison.

HARBISON. Good-bye, Billis. Oh, by the way, I never did get you in the brig...did I?

BILLIS. *(Laughing almost too heartily at his triumph.)* No! Ha-ha.

HARBISON. Oh, I forgot!

BILLIS. *(Still laughing.)* Forgot what, sir?

HARBISON. Your unit'll be on our ship. I'll be seeing all of you.

(Dismay from **BILLIS**, **STEWPOT**, *and the* **PROFESSOR**.*)*

Get the picture?

BRACKETT. Come on, Bill.

*(***BRACKETT*** and ***HARBISON*** exit.* ***BILLIS***, ***STEWPOT***, and the ***PROFESSOR*** pick up their gear and follow.)*

SHORE PATROLMAN. *(Entering.)* All right...let's start those trucks moving out – all units on the Company Street. We're ready to load you. All Nurses will board assigned planes – Seabees to embark on Carrier Six. All Marines to board LCTs. Any questions? MOVE OUT!

(The sounds of trucks roar. The music becomes march-like as the **MEN** *march off.* **NURSES** *in hospital uniform stand waving to the* **MEN** *and the* **NURSES** *in combat uniform who leave with them.)*

ALL.
A HUNDRED AND ONE
POUNDS OF FUN –

THAT'S MY LITTLE HONEY BUN!
GET A LOAD OF HONEY BUN TONIGHT!

HER HAIR IS BLONDE AND CURLY,
HER CURLS ARE HURLY-BURLY,
HER LIPS ARE PIPS!
I CALL HER HIPS:
"TWIRLY" AND "WHIRLY."
SHE'S MY BABY,
I'M HER PAP!
I'M HER BOOBY,
SHE'S MY TRAP!
I AM CAUGHT AND DON'T WANTA RUN,
'CAUSE I'M HAVIN' SO MUCH FUN WITH HONEY BUN!

(The **GROUPS** *are all dispersed.)*

Scene Twelve
Emile's Terrace

(The Company Street traveler opens to reveal the terrace of Emile's house. It is late afternoon – sunset; reddish light. The drone of planes can be heard. **JEROME** *stands on the table with* **NELLIE** *holding him.* **NGANA** *is beside her. All look off.)*

NELLIE. *(Pointing off.)* The big ones are battleships and the little ones are destroyers – or cruisers – I never can tell the difference.

(She looks up in the air.)

And what on earth are those?

JEROME. P-40s.

NELLIE. Oh, that's right. They're all moving out, you see, because, well…there's been a big change. They won't be around here much anymore, just off and on, a few of us. Did you understand anything I said? Vous ne comprenez pas?

NGANA. Oui, oui, nous comprenons.

*(***JEROME*** nods his head.)*

JEROME. Oui.

NELLIE. Now, while I'm down at the hospital, you've got to promise me to mangez everything – everything that's put before you on the table – sur le tobler. Sur la tobler?

NGANA. *(Smiling patiently.)* Sur la table.

NELLIE. *(Smiles, congratulating herself.)* Now come back here, Jerome, and sit down.

(She starts to place the **CHILDREN** *at the table, on which a tureen of soup and some bowls have been set. At this point,* **BUZZ ADAMS** *appears upstage – a weary figure. Behind him comes* **EMILE** *in a dirt-stained uniform, helmet, paratroop boots, and musette bag.*

> **ADAMS** *calls his attention to the planes droning above. Neither sees* **NELLIE** *nor the* **CHILDREN**. **NELLIE** *pushes the* **CHILDREN** *down on the bench as they playfully balk at being seated.)*

NELLIE. Ass-say-yay-voo.

[MUSIC NO. 48 "FINALE ULTIMO"]

> *(They sit.* **EMILE** *turns sharply at the sound of* **NELLIE**'s *voice.)*

Now you have to learn to mind me when I talk to you and be nice to me too. Because I love you very much. Now, mangez.

> *(***EMILE**'s *face lights up with grateful happiness.* **ADAMS** *knows it's time for him to shove off, and he does.* **NELLIE** *proceeds to ladle soup from the large tureen into three small bowls.)*

JEROME. *(Eyes twinkling mischievously.)* Chantez, Nellie.

NELLIE. I will not sing that song. You just want to laugh at my French accent.

> *(The* **CHILDREN** *put their spoons down – on strike.)*

All right, but you've got to help me.

NELLIE, NGANA & JEROME.
DITES-MOI
POURQOUI

> *(***NELLIE** *is stuck. The* **CHILDREN** *sing the next line without her.)*

NGANA & JEROME.
LA VIE EST BELLE,

NELLIE. *(Repeating quickly to catch up to them.)*
LA VIE EST BELLE

> *(Meanwhile,* **EMILE** *has crossed behind them.* **NELLIE** *is looking out front, not seeing him.*

Trying to remember the lyrics, she continues to sing with the **CHILDREN**.)

NELLIE, NGANA & JEROME.
DITES-MOI
POURQUOI

NELLIE. *(Turns to the* **CHILDREN**.*)* Pourquoi what?

(She sees **EMILE**.*)*

EMILE. *(Answering her.)*
LA VIE EST GAIE!

(**NELLIE** *gazes at him, hypnotized – her voice gone. The* **CHILDREN** *rush to embrace him.)*

NGANA & JEROME. Papa, Papa!

EMILE. *(Hugging both his* **CHILDREN** *as he continues singing.)*
DITES-MOI
POURQUOI,
CHERE MAD'MOISELLE –

*(***EMILE**, **NGANA**, *and* **JEROME** *bow.)*

EST-CE QUE
PARCE QUE
VOUS M'AIMEZ.

(The music continues. **EMILE** *kisses the* **CHILDREN**, *who then run back to their seats and begin drinking their soup.* **EMILE** *crosses to the table.)*

Mangez, Nellie.

*(***NELLIE** *sits.* **EMILE** *sits. The* **CHILDREN** *continue eating their soup. There is no bowl for* **EMILE**, *so* **NELLIE**, *barely taking her eyes off him, pushes the tureen across the table to him. Then, realizing there is no spoon for him, she hands him the ladle. They both start to drink, he with the ladle as a soup spoon, she with her own. They stare into each other's eyes and suddenly drop their spoons – she first – and*

finally clasp their hands downstage in front of the table and out of sight of the **CHILDREN** *as the music swells:)*

(The curtain falls.)

The End

Lightning Source UK Ltd.
Milton Keynes UK
UKHW020806141022
410463UK00011B/628

9 780573 708916